SILENT NIGHT

TWISTED HOLIDAYS

USA TODAY BESTSELLING AUTHOR

M.L. PHILPITT

AUTHOR'S NOTE

Silent Night is book 1 of Twisted Holidays, a series of standalone holiday romance novellas. They can be enjoyed in any order and will have no crossover between the characters/plots.

This book has content some people may find triggering. Please visit my website for the list of triggers and content warnings. Feel free to contact me with any questions. If you feel I have missed a trigger, please let me know.

Note, I'm Canadian. I write using Canadian/UK spelling. This means words will have U's in them, or double LL's. (colour, flavour, signalling, etc.) These are not typos.

Happy reading!

PLAYLIST

"Savage" by Bahari
"Saints" by Echos
"When the Darkness Comes" by Jeris Johnson
"Middle of the Night" by Elley Duhé
"Dangerous Hands" by Austin Giorgio
"Chills - Dark Version" by Mickey Valen & Joey Myron
"Take Me to Church" by Hozier
"I'm Yours" by Isabel LaRosa
"Wonderland" by Neoni
"I See Red" by Everybody Loves an Outlaw

For the romance readers who crave a bit of darkness this holiday season.

The Grinch snuck into people's homes to steal Christmas cheer.
Saint's gonna sneak into yours to steal you...
Ho, Ho, Ho, Merry Christmas...lock your windows.
Or don't.
No one's judging.

ONE
SAINT

GREED.

The dictionary defines the term as having an intense desire for something, often referring to wealth, power, or food.

No one ever admits this, since it'd be seen as a fault and they don't dare have any of those, but greed is the driving force behind people's actions. No one does shit for free anymore. It's how the rich stay rich and the poor stay poor. Everyone lives in their lanes, either striving for better or striving to continue as they are.

Once they're inside their designated lane, it's their desire for more that encourages them forward. In that, the rich showcase their wealth, gaining others' envy, and in turn, igniting their greed. When enticed to reach for more, behaviours get twisted, and they become shadows darkening humanity.

There's one time a year when people's greediness emerges stronger than ever. A time of year that they seem to relish in the feeling. When whiny kids beg for more toys, stores mark-up basically everything in stock, technology companies release the most updated cell phones, game consoles, and the like right in time to be snatched up, and organizations conveniently pop-up requesting money for others in these "difficult times."

One time of year that *celebrates* these behaviours.

Christmas.

Fucking *Christmas*.

I've always despised the holiday.

Perhaps it has something to do with it being the unfortunate day I was born, and every one of my twenty-six years on this planet, not one of them holds a positive memory. Adding to the fact that it was the very day that fifteen-year-old me got kicked out of the foster home I was in. Ironic that the day meant for celebrating with family was when I lost my chance at one.

And then there's the pain that comes with this stupid holiday. I'm on the outside, walking the streets as a shadow of society, forced to witness people get what they desire while my hopes and dreams have been long ground to dust, blown into the falling snow so re-sparking them would be impossible. No one pays attention to the ghost wandering around, even within the most affluent neighbourhoods, because they're all too selfish and too busy with their own lives to look twice. Too focused on opening their presents, so their gazes pass right over me.

It's always been like that, though. Once, it bothered me, but as I grew up, I realized how many benefits there were to being invisible. How easy it is to slip in and out of people's lives when they barely know you're there to begin with.

Not only their lives, but their homes too. After all, when I have nothing and they have everything, it's only fair they share.

It's why, a few days before Christmas, I'm walking through a neighbourhood filled with large houses—mini mansions essentially—with lawns blanketed with soft snow, strung with every holiday decoration one could stick on a property, and the expensive, luxury cars that are hidden within the multi-car garages. These are homes of wealthy people who leave every day for their equally-elaborate careers. Lawyers, doctors, businessmen, and such. Jobs that allow one to live like a king, unlike me, who picks up odd, menial jobs in each town I pass through.

These are the places where greed really shines as bright as the flashy, coloured bulbs attached to their roofs. When they already have all that money and everything a person could possibly want, yet for the holidays, they waste it on *more* fancy cars, the latest tech to replace the devices they got only the year before, and jewelry so grand it should be in a museum.

From the outside, they're also the homes that seem to have the most perfect Christmases, as I've witnessed over my years of doing this. The ones where they sing around a piano, drink hot chocolate, and lay out cookies for the imaginary creep who sneaks into their homes. The places where they sit around the tree on Christmas morning in pyjamas that cost more than most average-income families' entire wardrobe.

Greed is an interesting concept. Personally, I don't consider myself greedy when I rob them of their precious items. Especially considering, the next morning, they'll wake up to new ones, so they'll never miss the expensive painting on the wall. Or that vase on the random table in that random sitting room no one actually uses, but they insist on paying housekeepers to maintain. They don't need those items when they have much better uses.

Like funding my next few months of life.

I stop in front of the particular house I've chosen for this year; scoped out about a month ago, and spent the past few weeks studying, learning the ins and outs. The exterior walls are a light blue, and something about the shape of it, the decorations on the front lawn, it reminds me of the first house I ever stole from, four years ago.

That time was an accident, mixed with opportunity.

It soon became a lifestyle.

As I tread down the sidewalk with nothing better to do than let myself freeze in my thin, ripped jeans and even thinner jacket that I stole from someone's shopping cart earlier in the month, I remind myself I'm alive, and it's better than the fate of other people.

I don't know how or why I ended up in this neighbourhood of all places, but fuck, if anyone saw me they'd probably think I was out to rob them. The two or three storey houses scream wealth; a life I'll never experience. Long paved driveways, large bay windows displaying decorated trees, yards that are littered in holiday shit. These are the kinds of places that go all out for Halloween, and cover their property in flags for Canada Day, and even decorate for St. Patrick's Day. The places that can afford wasting their money on unimportant shit.

Nearby yelling draws my attention to a large blue house trimmed with bright, multi-coloured lights. There's a blown-up snowman on the front lawn, smiling and jolly and shit, but the noises coming from the family as they spill out onto the street are anything but joyful.

I stop, watching as a teenage girl screams at her parents. From the distance, she looks a bit younger than me, but I'd bet anything on this planet that she hasn't seen or done half the shit I have, especially as she's screeching at her family for what I assume is a stupid reason. Probably didn't buy her a freaking tiara in the right shade of gold or something else ridiculous. She runs down the road despite the fact it's negative twenty and she's wearing nothing thicker than a cardigan. Her parents trail after her, not bothering to lock their door.

I don't know what compels me, but once the family is out of view, I walk across the street, hoping all their neighbours are too busy in their own holiday cheer to bother paying the homeless guy entering this house any attention.

This is probably the worst idea I've ever had, but it's as if I'm watching myself from the outside, and I can't stop my feet from moving.

I slowly enter, passing the beige front door, half of which is a smoked glass window. Despite it being open and the icy outdoors spilling into the heated house, passing the doorway is like entering a shield, and penetrating it brings a wall of warmth that immediately begins thawing my body.

If the family returns now and calls the cops, I decide it's all worth it for this right here, right now: the tingling sensation as my body shifts from one extreme temperature to another. Besides, could this be considered breaking-in when they never shut the door? It's more like an invitation. Wholesome holiday cheer and all that.

I'll only stay a moment. Warm up and go.

As I'm turning for the door, a scent of...of...damn, I can't even describe the scent wafting from deeper in the house. It's like a mix of warm, baked cookies, a fireplace, and what I suspect is literal happiness—not that I know what that smells like—and I find myself heading down the hallway toward it.

Everything in this place is shiny and screams wealth. The finishings are a rich wood in a natural deep colour, but kept glossy so every visitors' gaze can't help but pay it attention. The foyer is huge, opening up to a grand staircase, like the ones in movies. The hallways are wider than I've ever seen, with high, vaulted ceilings, making the second floor look down on the first, like a balcony.

Stupidly, I venture farther into the house, knowing with every step I'm losing my argument if the family returns. It went from "sorry, I was cold because I'm homeless and you left your door open" to "sorry, I'm wandering your house for reasons I'm not sure."

I pass by an open doorway and peek inside, finding an office. The small space is lined with oak bookshelves, only one of them actually storing books. The books are leather-bound with black or gold script on the spines, giving little indication of the words inside, almost like they're only for decoration. The other shelves hold small, ornamental items. Pointless junk.

The bulky desk is home to a metal lamp and a closed laptop, a leather executive chair tucked into it. The massive painting hanging behind the desk is what draws my attention.

It's of a woman sitting on a chair, her smile wide as she faces forward. Her dark hair is done up, her pale dress unwrinkled. A man stands behind her, his hand resting on her shoulder in a claiming manner. He isn't smiling, but his eyes shine with pride. Beside him is a girl, no older than the one I watched bolt down the road, like this portrait was commissioned recently.

I find myself immediately captivated by her and the way she smirks at the camera, mischievous even in her parents' presence. Dark curls are unruly around her face, and she slouches, the opposite from her parents' rigid positions, like she's saying with her body that she doesn't want to be in the picture.

This must be the family who just ran off. It's an interesting portrait. Nearly perfect, but with a lengthier study, it's obvious there's trouble in paradise. The parents and their stiff, formal positions indicate wanting not to be near one another, and the daughter obviously has no care about this family picture. Was probably forced into it.

I wonder what caused them to yell at one another outside. Clearly, the problems the portrait depicts carries into their realities.

As I turn away, my eye catches on something particularly shiny, encased in a glass case. A jewel-encrusted dagger propped on a stand. It must be worth a lot, to be in a case, stored in an office like this and away from visitors' eyes. Even if it's not "a lot" by these people's standards, it probably is to mine.

I should leave, but what's one more sin? I wonder how long it'll take the man in the painting to notice it's gone.

Before I debate too long, I open the case and slip my hand inside to—

"What are you doing? Who are you?"

I look up to see the girl from the painting, her curls as unruly as the portrait, her arms crossed over her chest as she watches me watch her, piecing together exactly what I'm doing.

I rip my hand away, eyes sweeping the small space for escape. She's blocking the only exit, which means remembering what my excuse was going to be if the family found me here.

"H-hey, sorry. I won't hurt you."

Her dark eyes scan me, landing on my thin clothing and the holes in my jeans. With her examination, she makes her own judgement, but unlike so many others, it doesn't harshen her otherwise soft face. A sort of pitying smile graces her lips and she shrugs.

"*I believe you.*" *She jerks her chin to the case.* "*Honestly, take it. Serves the asshole right. But they're, like, minutes away. I turned through some-one's yard to lose them, but they'll figure it out soon. So if you're planning to steal it, you should probably take it and go now.*"

She's letting me go free? Even better: she's letting me steal from her house?

It might be a trick but being homeless, starving, and freezing says otherwise, so I wrap my hand around the hilt of the dagger and shove it into an inner pocket of my jacket before moving toward her, my steps slow so she doesn't freak out.

I stop in front of her, staring down, seeing now she truly can't be that much younger than me. Older than a teenager but not by much. Slightly older than the painting on the wall, I now see. As I make my own assess-ment, she's obviously coming up with one too, her gaze scanning my face. She's the closest I've been to another person in a long time and it's borderline unnerving to be studied so closely.

She jolts before stepping back. I want to know what's in her head, but considering I'm a thief standing in her house and her parents are only minutes away, it's not the time for conversation.

"*Thank you,*" *I whisper as I pass her, and before I can understand what I'm doing, I lift a hand to her cheek, stroking calloused fingers along skin belonging to a girl meant for the lifestyle this house suggests. For once, I'm not annoyed by this fact, but enthralled. She's so fucking soft, but before I grow addicted to what I can't afford, I take off, down the hall and back outside into the cold before cutting around the back of her house and well out of sight, my stolen object safely in my pocket.*

I never got the chance to thank that girl for fighting with her family that day. She didn't only give me a few minutes of warmth, but she also introduced me to a new life. Pawn shops ask few questions and that dagger paid out a pretty penny. Enough to put up two months' rent on a rundown apartment and managed to stay warm enough for the remainder of those coldest winter months before skipping town.

7

That was four years ago, and for the past three of them, I found myself in similar neighbourhoods every holiday season. It's easy to slip inside when back doors are so often left unlocked or easily pickable. I've learned to choose a house and study it and its occupants for the weeks leading up to the holidays, learning their patterns, scoping what I can of their valuables to determine if it'll be profitable.

The house I stand in front of is home to a middle-aged couple. All week, they've been unloading bags upon bags of presents after coming home from whichever white-collar jobs they have. They use Christmas-time to fund their incessant need for more material items by spending all that they make at those very jobs. *Idiots.* Unlike so many other families in the area, they don't even have the excuse of wanting to spoil their snot-nosed kids—which only causes children to grow up as greedy, selfish, and spoiled as the adults around them—because they have none that I've seen.

Either way, I've seen the labels on the bags they carry inside. Instead of stealing art or a valuable object, I could rob any one of the gifts beneath the tree and be set for a while.

In two nights, I'll return.

In three, I'll be gone from this town.

TWO
HAYLEY

ARRIVING to an empty house on the night before Christmas Eve is a slap to the face. After Mom begged me over and over for the past three months to visit this year, I begrudgingly agreed, thinking—*assuming*—my idiotic fault apparently—that coming for the holidays would mean *she'd be here.* Instead, only minutes before my flight took off, she left a voice mail that I only received *after* deboarding the plane and turning off airplane mode. She cancelled our plans last-minute so she and stepfather number two could fly off into the sun for some tropical vacation.

I would have hopped on the next flight out—if they weren't completely booked up. Which makes sense, considering which day it is. The earliest available seat was on the twenty-seventh, which means I'm stuck in a house that isn't mine, in a town I'm unfamiliar with, for the next five days.

I can't even be surprised by this. Mom's flightily, bitchy behaviour is typical; something I've lived with far too long. Last year, I remained in my dorms with all the other students who opted not to go home, or didn't have a place to go home to, while she gallivanted around finding said second stepfather. Last year, I wanted a happy, peaceful, and quiet holiday for once, with only us two, but she insisted on needing a new man in her life, and this need just couldn't wait a damn week.

"You wanted a nice holiday. I got us one," was her main argument to get me to visit this year.

She totally missed the "only us" part of my request, which has become a mistake I'll never make again.

The taxi pulls up to a house that reminds me of the one I grew up in, because once again, Mommy Dearest found herself a rich husband, the same as Dad. Ever since they divorced when I was eighteen, she's basically tried to replace Dad with duller, older versions. Stepdad number one was a piece of work. At least the new guy, Dean, doesn't slap her ass at the dinner table in front of a room full of guests.

I'd only been here once before, for her and Dean's wedding, and it was one time too many.

I toss an entire stack of twenties onto the front seat of the cab because it's Dean's cash since he insisted on paying for all my travel expenses, so I gift it all away, and the driver helps me with my suitcase.

"Thanks, and Merry Christmas," I tell the man, imagining him soon going home to his family. There's a picture of himself, a woman, and three kids taped to his dash that he glanced at every red light.

"You too," he replies in a tone cheerier than I can handle right now, but it's not this stranger's fault my mother turned yet another holiday to shit.

With my bag in tow, I turn toward the house, for once thankful that Dean gave me a key to the place and a room for when I visit, insisting I drop in whenever. Of course, Mom sent me an evil glare that *dared* me to disrupt her peaceful new life when he said that.

Dean isn't a bad guy. He's just not Dad.

Mind you, post-divorce Dad took off to Europe to "restart" and only checks in by phone every few months. The last time I heard from him was the start of November. Maybe tomorrow, I'll get a call, or at the very least, a text.

I trudge up the stone walkway scattered with freshly fallen snow, trying to convince myself this is no different than if I remained alone in my apartment, since I no longer live on campus. The building would probably be quiet, since the majority of renters are students too, and most off to their families' places.

With the key, I unlock the door and enter the dark house, flicking on the foyer's light. It illuminates the open space; the oversized closet probably storing all Mom's ridiculously overpriced jackets, a padded bench that screams *decoration only* because if I know Mom, she expects guests to balance as they put on their shoes. Beside the front door is a shoe mat, a single pair of men's boots on it. Likely Dean's, and I'm shocked he got away with leaving his items in the open like this. Mom insists on hiding "mess."

I kick off my snowy shoes, not bothering to place them on the mat. The snow will soon melt in the house's heat and mixed with dirt from outside, it'll turn to mud that'll drip onto Mom's shiny floors. Serves her right. She'll come home to a mess.

At the base of the carpeted staircase, I abandon my suitcase and wander toward the kitchen, flicking on lights as I go. The kitchen is full of fancy, industrial appliances because Dean is a chef, and if I'm honest with myself, I was looking forward to his home-cooked Christmas dinner. I haven't had one since before Mom and Dad divorced, and if Dean cooks as well as Mom claims, then it could have been a turkey to remember.

Chances are, a lot of takeout is getting ordered between now and my flight home, unless I figure out how to use the fancy stove with one too many knobs. Maybe I'll try anyway, and if I burn the place down, oh well. Guess they should have been here.

It's with those annoyed, grim thoughts, I enter the dim kitchen, stopped by the lone figure leaning against the counter, a glass in his hand, and a bottle of brandy—probably stupidly expensive—resting beside him. He turns, spotting me, and a pleased smirk spreads across his face.

Fuck. Now I wish I chose to hole up in the airport for the next few days because literally anywhere would be better than here, alone with *him.* How the hell did I not even consider that he might be visiting this year too? I wonder if it's too late to consider booking a hotel room for the week—even if the likelihood in finding availability is slim-to-none.

My stepbrother's messy grin matches everything else about his demeanor. The rumpled suit, the wild hair, the evil glint in his eyes as the lights hanging over the island counter separating us catches on them. Right now, I love that granite island more than anything.

"Ha, this is too fuckin' good!" One finger lifts from the hand gripping the glass and gestures toward me. "They fucked you over too."

"Bentley." It's almost a gasp. A combination of shock and discomfort as I force my body still because he's like a fox who'll sniff out my fear, and the last thing I want is to become his prey.

My stepbrother tips his head in a mock greeting. From the very first meeting, I never liked him. First off, who names their son after a car? Secondly, despite the fact we were at a forced dinner with our parents as they tried to bring both sides together, he stared at me like we were alone. Leered would be more like it. It was chilling, sending prickles down my spine as he gawked at me, like he was hoping to make *me* his dessert that night.

For that reason, I declined the offer to accompany our parents home and skipped out early.

The second time I interacted with him was at their wedding, months after that initial dinner. They had a "small"—Mom's words—gathering of about two hundred people, but I ended up being grateful for every single one of them. Whenever Bentley tried to approach me, I'd run the opposite way, limiting our time together to when we had to walk down the aisle. Mom was pissed when I avoided the one and only dance I was technically mandated to share with him. The aisle involved enough touching for the year, thanks.

"Hayley," Bentley greets back. "And here, Christmas just got better."

"Yeah. Great." It's not great; it's horrible, but my fake smile hopes to ease the tension.

Bentley turns and grabs another glass from the cabinet before pouring a large amount of liquor into it and sliding it across the island toward me. I take it, accepting his peace offering, but drink nothing more than a tiny sip, preferring to remain sober around him.

"So, what happened? How'd our parents fuck you over?"

"Mom convinced me to come this year. When I got off the plane, I got her voice mail saying she and your father are skipping the holidays to go down south 'til the twenty-eighth. What's your story?"

He scoffs and refills his own glass before taking another shot, and I wonder how many of those he's already had. "Sounds like your mom. No offense, but she's a piece of work."

"None taken."

"Dad basically played the same bullshit game with me. After denying him a dozen times, I finally agreed, and look..." His hands spread dramatically to the side. "I'm fuckin' here, aren't I? Arrived a couple hours ago to an empty house. Messaged him, and he said he and your mother took off for a last-minute vacation. At least your mother had the decency to give you a bit of a head's up. I had to chase my father for answers."

Dislike of Bentley aside, there's relief in knowing we both got screwed over.

"Wonderful," I mutter. "Well, I'm stuck here 'til the twenty-seventh because it was the first flight I could get on, and they'll be back the day after. By then, you'll have to return to work." I'm assuming that his job in finance is demanding because Mom claims he's always too busy to come for dinner. "So you may as well head out now." The plea in my tone must be unmissable. He lives about an hour away, so he can get home by bedtime.

Bentley grins around his glass. "See, when I showed up, that was the plan. I was going to drink myself stupid on Dad's expensive shit, pass out 'til morning, and then drive home tomorrow. But now..." His eyes rake me, settling on the low dip of my top. "I might stick around for a few days. Gotta protect baby sis and all that."

Fuck. "Please." Ideally my scoff hides the shakiness in my tone. "We're basically the same age."

"Still older," he argues.

"I'm also not a child in need of protection, so I'll be fine. Go home." *Please go home. Right now. Drive off. Leave me.*

His eyes rake over me again, his salacious smirk making me want to curl up and die. "Nah, Christmas is looking up for the first time in years." He drops his glass to the counter with a thud I feel through my entire form. "It's cold out there, so we'll remain warm and cozy in here. I'd be a dick to leave you alone on the holidays like our parents did."

No, it'd be your greatest gift. "It's fine," I urge as a last stab. "I'll be fine."

He comes around the counter and I manage a tiny step back. Small enough, hopefully he doesn't notice, but based on the way his gaze flicks to my feet and back, he did. He takes a larger step this time, his grin telling me he doesn't care about my attempted escape.

"Bentley, I'm tired and not in the mood."

He stops with only inches between us, looking down at me, the same way I picture he does his clients. "Who said you had to be in the mood?"

Why did that sound like a greater threat?

"Bentley," I say in a firm warning tone.

His malicious stare breaks and he bops me on the nose as he continues by me. "Relax, lil' sis. I'm just fuckin' with you. Hungry? I'll order us something."

"Pizza's fine," I reply to his retreating back. Until he stops playing nice, or whatever his version of that is, I'll be cordial at the very least. Enough to get past Christmas and get the hell out of here.

Bentley makes a sign with his hand to show me he's heard me. Once he's gone for a few minutes, I abandon the kitchen with a sigh to lug my bag upstairs. On my way to the foyer, I pass him seated in the luxurious living room on one of the couches that no one actually sits in, the massive tree in front of the even larger window, talking on the phone. This house is like something on TV, and yet, everything Mom for some reason chases.

Skipping by before he has a chance to say anything, I drag my heavy suitcase up the carpeted steps and to the room Dean assigned me last year. With a regretful stare at the door across from mine, I realize I'll have to spend the night directly across from Bentley.

I shiver. Hopefully for everything he says, he actually is fucking with me. That his implied threats are simply that: threats, and he'll stay on his side of the hallway.

I open the door to my room, praying to see a lock on the inside, but there's unfortunately none. I drop my suitcase in the centre of the decently sized room, only equipped with minimal furniture, exactly as a guest room would be. A queen-sized bed covered in a red comforter is in the centre, a nightstand on either side. Across is a dresser I suspect to be empty, with a flatscreen TV on top. It's like a hotel room, which is essentially what this place feels like.

I crouch down to unzip my suitcase, pulling out the first lounge clothing I find, ones that'll cover me even more than what I'm presently wearing. I stand, pulling my shirt, gross from travelling, off and toss it to the floor when the slow clapping makes its way to me.

Shit, I forgot to close the door.

I spin, clutching my new shirt to my chest, finding Bentley leaning against the doorframe, his arms crossed over his chest, one foot over the other. He winks when I face him before pushing off the frame and entering my room, bearing down on me like the predator I suspect him to be.

"I came up to let you know pizza will be here in about twenty minutes, and certainly wasn't expecting this." He doesn't hide the fact that his eyes graze every inch of me that is bare, and I try my best to spread my shirt to cover more of my skin, all without lifting my arms.

17

"Can't you see I'm busy?"

"Busy," he repeats with a smirk. He finishes his agonizing study by glancing toward my suitcase. "*Please* tell me these are your gifts to me." He bends, retrieving a pair of red, silk panties from my bag, and dangles them in front of my face.

My face probably goes as red as the underwear for how warm it suddenly gets, partly from embarrassment but mostly from rage. I reach for them, but he's quick to snap his arm up, avoiding my hand. It forces me to stretch, but I quickly back down after weighing the pros and cons of getting them back. Get them back and probably show him more of my chest in the process versus letting him win and being able to stay covered.

He brings them back down slowly, holding them slightly off to the side so he can quickly lift them away again if I go for them. "These. I want these for my present."

"Keep them," I grit my teeth. Anything to get him to leave.

"Nah, you're missing an important element." He bends slightly, lining his face up with mine so I'm forced to see the malice glinting playfully in his eyes. "I want these on you. I want to remove them myself."

"Ugh." I snap my hand toward the silk again, but this time, he lets me have it, laughing. I shove away from him, keeping the panties, which now feel violated, close to me. "You're disgusting, Bentley."

He shrugs. "What? We're not actually related."

"Bentley—"

"God, you're so fun to fuck with. Easy too." He rolls his eyes, spinning on his heel as he heads back for the door. "Anyway, pizza will be here soon, so dress. Or don't. I don't mind either way."

He shuts the door before I find something to throw at him.

THREE
SAINT

PEOPLE ARE DUMB. Instead of the house's owners having a quiet conversation, they left that morning, multiple suitcases in tow as they loaded up in their BMW with more numbers on the trunk than I care to memorize, and the wife all but screaming their plans.

"I can't wait to be on the beaches of Mexico by tomorrow!"

Luckily, I was nearby, continuing to stalk the house to ensure my Christmas Eve plans to break in go off without a hitch. But now, they handed me the gold key. Why wait until tomorrow when I can sneak in today, steal what I can, and escape? They don't have surveillance cameras; I've peeked through their windows enough times to check, so maybe I'll even camp out for a day or two, enjoying the warmth that privilege and wealth provides. Or I'll take what I can tonight and return tomorrow for more, like the Grinch. Only, I won't feel bad about stealing their Christmas when they're off to have a different, tropical one after announcing it to the damn world.

It's like they're *begging* to be robbed. Lucky for them, I'll grant them that wish.

I return after the sun drops, skirting my way to the other side of the road and against the house, sticking to the shadows. They have a back door that leads to their kitchen, so it'll be less conspicuous to jimmy that lock and slip inside.

The lights on the neighbours' houses are dimmed, allowing me to sneak in undetected. It's too chilly outside for people to be hanging around too. All are tucked inside, presumably asleep, since it's past midnight. They need their rest so their greed can begin kicking off tomorrow, Christmas Eve, which is only an appetizer for the main course: the day after.

With a bobby pin and knife, I unlock the back door easily. Despite all these people's money, they never have enough sense to install security cameras or better locks. Well, a few houses do, and they're the ones I stay away from.

Warmth greets me as I enter. I step inside quietly, even though there's no one here, peering through the dark before flicking on a light. A grand kitchen greets me. Shiny appliances, rows of spices on a rack above the counter, pots and pans hanging from hooks in the ceiling.

My stomach growls, reminding me of the last time I ate: last night. Much too long. If the residents of this place are gone on their sudden vacation, surely they forgot to clean everything out, which means by eating their food, I'm doing them a favour. Not like they'll miss it.

Food. Warmth. And a comfortable bed for a day or two. Yep, I've chosen well.

I tread through the space, heading for the fridge first, suddenly eager to eat something other than whatever I steal. Fresh fruit, for one. I long for the taste of an apple again.

The fridge light illuminates the room, but as I turn around, the room grows even brighter from the overhead lights, and by the time I register what's happening, it's too late.

"Who the fuck are you and why are you in my house?"

I freeze, slowly unpeeling my fingers from the fridge's handle, watching as food literally slips through my hands, and turn around, keeping the knife in view.

Standing in the entrance to the kitchen is a woman, probably around my age. Her dark curls are a mess, partially bound up on her head with more strands falling to her shoulder than what seems to have made it into the elastic. Her full, pouty lips are parted, halfway between fear and shock as she stands, frozen, her hand still on the light switch. Her eyes pin me from across the room and I'm taken right back to the first house I ever robbed, when a girl found me before allowing me to steal from her family.

The similarities of these two nights are disturbing. I slowly pace toward her, watching with a bit of a thrill as her eyes widen like a doe faced with a wolf.

When I'm within six feet from her, before she turns and bolts, I catch something beneath that fear: a bravado that's kept her going. A hard swallow before she lifts her chin slightly, facing down what could very well be her death. She's bold...just like she was when finding me four years ago.

"*You,*" I breathe.

There's no fucking way—no *chance*—that this woman is the same girl from four years ago. But there's too many similarities in her messy hair, her eyes, even her stance. Like a ghost having popped up.

She blinks, jerking back before blinking again, this time slower. She leans forward, her eyes studying over my face. "Oh my god, it's *you.*" She glances at the knife in my grip and licks her bottom lip in what I assume to be a nervous twitch. "Have a habit of breaking into people's homes?"

"Yes," I reply, gauging how she'll manage the truth. "Ever since that day."

"Right." She huffs, almost laughs, her tense gaze locked on the knife still, so I flick it shut and slip it into my pocket before showing her both my palms are now empty.

"I won't hurt you, I swear."

I should because if she wanted to, she could identify me to the police. Of course, I'd already be on the first bus out of town, but when the rich want revenge, the cops fall all over themselves to make shit happen. My face will be plastered on the news through every town, city, and perhaps even province nearby.

Seeing her now, this stranger whose name I don't know, I can't hurt her. There's no plausible reason, but the thought of harming her at all makes me want to harm myself. Especially when she blinks again, and those fucking doe eyes of hers look too trusting, too innocent. Brown and green swirl together into a deep amber, a colour I'd happily let myself drown in.

She's definitely innocent. She screams it in the way she gazes at me. It's almost stupid because she looks naïve...soft...in a way making me want to protect her, which is fucked up because I'm the only monster here. I wonder if her skin is still as soft as when I last touched her, but I doubt she'd accept me stroking her cheek again. She's grown in the four years, as I have, so presumably she's found some common sense during that time, and a stranger standing in her home is quite obviously a threat.

But clearly she doesn't have a ton, since instead of screaming at me to leave or cowering in fear, she simply murmurs, "I believe you."

"You shouldn't considering I've broken into your home." Twice now.

Suddenly, my face is closer to her, enough I can smell the sweet scent drifting from her. She's probably wearing a perfume that costs what one of those gifts beneath her Christmas tree is worth, but for once, I'm not turned off by the thought of the cash spent on the quality scent as I gravitate toward her. It's an aroma calling me to her, as though to lead me to danger.

"Maybe you're not the scariest monster in this place." She smirks and while I'm working to figure out if she's fucking with me or not, she says, "I'm assuming you've come to rob us again."

I lick my bottom lip, my gaze dropping over her form. She's dressed in sleep shorts, her legs a delicious tan, and a silk tank, her breasts on full display. I can't recall the last time I was attracted to a woman. A life on

24

the move doesn't exactly bring many opportunities. Usually, it's women who run in the same circles I do. Those who ask few questions and just want a good time to make a night pass. But never someone like this girl. Someone who's as fine as the house we stand inside. As delicate as the crystal glasses in the glass cabinets nearby. Someone I certainly can't afford to touch, let alone think about. Someone who makes my cock twitch beneath my jeans, the need to feel her—even simply a brush of her skin—making it difficult to think about anything else.

The differences between us are striking. Her in her silk, me in thin, stolen cotton clothing. She smells like flowers from the most remote parts of the world, while my last shower was this morning in a community rec centre with plain soap. Her head is tipped up to watch me, yet she's well above me in terms of a social hierarchy.

"Yep." I go for honesty because at this point, I'm curious to see how far I can push her before she cracks and runs away screaming. A girl like this won't last long in the company of someone like me. Someone who doesn't wear polo shirts and golf for fun. Someone who'd love nothing more but to dirty her up.

She glances over my shoulder and around the kitchen. "See anything you like? Other than our food."

You.

When I don't answer right away, she passes me, her arm brushing my jacket like she wasn't just in a standoff with someone who could have killed her and run off with whatever I want. She heads for the fridge, yanking the doors open, and I'm too busy staring at her ass to pay her task any attention. Her shorts are...well, *short*, letting me see the curve of her ass.

"Hm...leftover pizza?"

Fuck, I can't even remember the last time I ate pizza. The thought of it is almost as delicious as the idea of spreading her out on the counter and taking my meal from her cunt, which I'm positive would be a dessert unlike any other.

25

"Um." I cough, clearing my throat—and my head from the thoughts. "Sure."

She slides out a pizza box and drops it onto the counter, like feeding a criminal is the most natural thing in the world for her. She retrieves a plate, which suggests she wants me to eat like she does: dignified, and not out of the box like an animal salivating over the pepperoni slices.

She leans on the counter across from me, propping herself on her elbows, giving me a clear sight down the front of her top. *Jesus.* I nearly choke on the first bite of the cold but delicious pizza.

"So this is a coincidence." She tilts her head and gestures between us. "What are the chances?"

I finish chewing before answering, figuring a fancy girl like her prefers men who have manners. "Apparently pretty good. You've moved from the other town."

She rolls her eyes. "This isn't even my house. The place we first met was my parents' but since then, they've divorced and my mom has been through two other marriages." She circles her hand. "House of stepdad number two."

Yet another of many reasons I should despise this woman. She's had three different families, numerous parents, while I've barely had one.

"Where do you live then?" I ask, the question slipping out before I can stop myself.

Surely, common sense would mean not to disclose her location.

She narrows her eyes slightly, licking her bottom lip, and I find myself compelled by the tiny slip of her tongue. "Away from here, at school."

Fancy girl gets to go to a fancy university for a proper education. Another thing so far out of my reach, not that I've ever aspired to go. Barely finishing high school was enough.

"Do you have a habit of feeding strangers who've broken in? Or letting them go with expensive decorations you don't own?"

She tips her head, curls slipping from the top of her head toward her shoulder and I tighten my fist before accidentally reaching to replace them. "Just one apparently." She smirks at her own joke. "You know, it took six months for Dad to even realize it was gone. What'd you do with it anyway?"

"Pawned it. Made a decent chunk of cash from it."

"Good. I'm sure you made better use of it than he could have."

I should be insulted by that statement, if she wasn't so correct.

"Why aren't you scared of me?" I ask after another bite.

Her lips twitch, fighting a smile. "If you wanted to harm me, you'd have done it already."

She's not wrong about that. "Still, you should be scared. I'm a stranger in your home and all."

"I was. Then I wasn't. Besides, maybe I enjoy the danger." The brown in her eyes glints in the hanging lights, suggesting more than she means. Before I can ask and let myself go down that potentially wrong path, I say something else.

"I heard your parents shouting about leaving on vacation this morning, so I figured I'd do the job sooner than later. Get in, get out." I skip over the fact I was also going to camp here for a couple days.

She snorts, straightening to position her palms flat on the counter. Her tank is tight around her nipples, the little buds all but begging for my attention. My fucking Christ, how's a man supposed to eat around her when eating *her* is all I can now think about? She's entirely too innocent. If she wasn't, she wouldn't dare be flashing someone who could easily take what's being offered on a silver damn platter.

If only I was that kind of man.

"Yeah, well, the assholes forgot to inform me until I landed."

So her school's far enough away she flew here. Information to file away, though there's too many schools in the country to pinpoint which one she goes to.

"Rude," I comment since I don't know what else to say. She's complaining about being in this huge house alone? Warm, comfortable, with plenty of food? See—greedy.

Suddenly, I want to be greedy too. I want to take more than a few valuables.

I want *her*.

Her on this counter, spread out, a Christmas feast for the taking.

A crack from down the hall has her tensing, her attention going to the hallway behind us. When it happens again, she curses and wide eyes pin me. Before I realize she's moved, she's yanking on my thin jacket, tugging me off the barstool and toward a skinny door that's encased with a smoked glass beside the fridge.

She yanks it open, hissing, "Get in, shut up, don't move," and then closes it.

I stop it with a finger before it can click shut, pushing it open half an inch for a limited view. She moves away from the door as another person enters the kitchen.

FOUR
HAYLEY

BENTLEY TREADS INTO THE KITCHEN, his hair askew from sleep, his chest bare, wearing only a pair of pyjama pants. "What are you doing up? It's one a.m."

"Got thirsty," I admit the truth. It is why I originally came down... before finding the stranger in our house. The stranger presently hiding three feet behind me in the pantry.

Bentley glances at the open pizza box.

"And hungry," I supply. "Period cravings and all." That part's a lie, but it's meant to deter him from whatever reason he's slowly pacing across the kitchen toward me.

Bentley stops close to me, his feet almost touching mine. With a tilt of my neck, I stare him down, exactly as he's doing to me, trying to show him he can't scare me. "Why don't I believe you?"

I shrug, inching away from him. "Because you have trust issues."

"Hm." He reaches out slowly, but I avoid his touch by stepping back again. He follows, and we complete this dance until my back hits the fridge right beside the pantry. It's cracked open a fraction, meaning I forgot to shut it completely, but I avoid letting my gaze linger, not to draw Bentley's attention toward it and the person hiding inside.

Thankfully, he's too distracted with trying to intimidate me. He slides his finger along my tank top's strap, lingering around the swell of my breast. I'm quick to smack him away, but he's quicker to position both his arms beside my head and press closer to me.

"Bentley," I say in a warning tone.

"Relax," he whispers. "You're so fucking uptight. I can be the man to loosen you right up though."

"God, you make me sick." I jerk my arms until gaining control of them again and shove his chest. He backs up, grinning.

"And you're so easy to mess with. Like I said before, we're not related so there's nothing wrong with it. Anyway, enjoy your...whatever it is you're doing. I'm going back to bed. If you get cold later, feel free to join me in my bed. I'll keep you nice and toasty."

Ew.

With a final mocking salute, he spins on his heel and stalks out of the kitchen. I wait, pressed against the fridge, until I hear him far enough away to assume he's gone back upstairs.

I force a few deep breaths, shaky now from my interaction with him. It's funny how he makes me more nervous than the criminal hiding in the pantry.

The criminal I should have had removed immediately, whether with Bentley's help or the cops. Or both. After all, what else should one do when finding someone breaking into their house?

When coming down and finding him rooting through the kitchen, I was struck with the immediate fear but played it off casually, figuring he'd be like old schoolyard bullies. Avoid showing fear to not empower them. But then the stranger turned around and I saw who it was.

Still, I can't believe the coincidence.

For the weeks following when I found him skulking around in my childhood home, hand gripping one of Dad's valuables, I thought about him. Even then, there was something alluring about him that I never made sense of. It wasn't until later analyzing my interest in guys that it all made sense.

That same Christmas morning sparked many changes in my life. Not only meeting him, but the downfall of my parents. I learned my mother's secret, which was the initial fracture of our family. When she and Dad began arguing, the holiday was completely ruined. Even today, the shouting echoes with that horrible memory, and no Christmas has been happy since. Dad's rage was justified to Mom's actions, but I yelled at them to stop fighting; to leave it alone for the day that was supposed to have pleasant memories. I'd threatened to run away if they didn't stop, and accidentally let it slip where I'd be—with the boyfriend they didn't know about.

He was two years older than me and ran with a rough group of people. Now looking back on that time in my life, I recognize he wasn't the best choice for me. Or legal. But at the time, I was enthralled with him because he was so "free," even though he had no life aspirations to do anything actually useful. He and his buddies hung around one of their parents' basements, smoking dope, playing video games, and getting drunk day in and day out. To stupid eighteen-year-old me, he was thrilling. Fun. Everything I thought I wanted. He gave me attention when my parents were always too busy. Filled in the loneliness left in me when Dad was constantly working and Mom chose shopping and spa days with her friends—and her side relationship apparently—over spending time with me.

When I meant to run to his place, I ended up turning around and heading back home instead. That's when I discovered the stranger in Dad's office. He looked scared and cold. His clothing looked fairly new but too thin for the winter weather. Considering how I took off in only a t-shirt and cardigan, yeah, it was definitely thick coat weather. He had dark marks beneath his eyes, making me wonder when he last slept. There was something so...lost...in his gaze that called to me. A loneliness I recognized all too well in myself.

Since I was an asshole brat who was pissed at her parents, I let him go with the decorative dagger I knew cost quite a bit. For weeks afterwards, I wondered where my dark stranger—a nickname I gave him—went to. *Who* he was.

That's when, I realized I was drawn to the dark and dangerous ones. The ones who make me *feel* something other than this emptiness I so often do. Him, the college guy I was dating, and the few boyfriends after him. The ones who should have cops called on them, rather than doing what I am.

Taking a deep breath and turning toward the pantry, I figure it's a good enough time for the stranger to come out now that Bentley's back in bed. Now, I need to get him gone, though I haven't figured out how to do so yet.

"You can—"

Hands reach for me, dragging me inside the pantry instead, yanking the door shut. My back hits the shelves as a large body presses me into them, his hair tickling my cheek, his growl coasting over my skin and straight to my insides.

"Who the fuck is he?"

Jealousy pours off him in thick waves, if that wasn't so ridiculous considering he doesn't even know me. Hands grip my wrists, and his nose skirts the side of my face, following a similar path Bentley took. Unlike him, the red flags that should be erecting, don't.

"My stepbrother."

He strokes a finger along the same tank strap that Bentley did, and with it, goosebumps sprout. I bite down on the small shiver, not wanting him to see how he's affecting me. His touch eviscerates Bentley's unwanted one and I could happily let him touch me everywhere.

"Why didn't you tell him I was in here?" With the lack of light in the pantry, his expression is shielded, but *god* do I want to see him.

"Because then we'd have a problem on our hands."

"We" he repeats with emphasis, a bit of a chuckle in the single word. "We're a *we* now?"

"Um." I didn't mean it like that. "I, uh, just meant..."

"Relax."

I do immediately, his command latching onto a forbidden, dark part of me that's more than happy to obey this stranger.

His cheek brushes mine, his hairs tickling the side of my face again as he leans closer. I'm a statue of indecision, knowing I should push him off of me, but not wanting to either. He could very well kill me now, go after Bentley, and rob us. We'd be ruled as a murder scene and if he's good, he could get away with it too.

His hands encircle my wrists, pinning them to my sides. "That's twice now you've saved me when you could have gotten me in trouble. Starting to think you're full of bad ideas, girl."

"Maybe." Wouldn't be the first time. "You talk like you *want* to get in trouble."

He chuckles, his breath blowing down the front of my tank, and fuck, I'm thankful he can't see how my body reacts. "I want you to be smart and have some sense. Letting a stranger roam your house, touch you..." To emphasize his words, his grip tightens. "Eat your food is a bad idea."

"I know," I breathe, my lungs feeling seconds from exploding. I tilt my face slightly, catching the glimmer from his eyes as he meets my gaze. "What's your name?"

I half-expect him to avoid answering, but he replies, "Saint." It was too quick an answer, so I feel he's telling the truth.

"Why do I get the sense you're no saint?"

"Because I'm not." He pulls back slightly, the shadowed version of him tipping his head. "Saints are good guys, and baby, I'm everything but. They worship at altars, while I'm ready to make you mine."

Good fucking Christ. He—Saint—needs to get out of here, out of my life before I make a huge fucking mistake. That's what he'd be. The criminal sneaking into my house, who claims he won't hurt me sounds like a lie waiting to happen.

"What's your name, sweet girl?"

For the first time all night, I hesitate. It's silly really because it's only my name. Without a last name to go along with it, he can't really gain anything from it. But it feels different. More intimate if he knows who I am.

He takes my long pause the correct way. "Not going to tell me? Finally you're being smart. I like that, though it's a shame I won't know the name of the girl who's saved me twice. That's more than anyone else has ever done for me."

That comment makes my heart pang. He sounds so lonely, so lost. "Why do you keep saying I've saved you?"

His hands release my wrists, and one trails up the inside of my arm as he replies, "Because you could have locked me in your father's office until your parents got back, and then had me arrested. Tonight, you could have fought back, told your stepbrother about me hiding in your pantry, called the cops yourself...so many options, but you didn't do any of them."

"Night's not over."

He chuckles, the sound way too dark, dangerous, and delicious for my libido. He's still touching me, still standing close. I need to breathe something that isn't him—my newest bad idea.

"I want out of here."

Saint, for all he's said, keeps his initial word about not hurting me and immediately backs away, pushing open the pantry door. He steps out first, not meeting my eyes as I follow, walking to the other side of the room, breathing in much-needed air.

"Stay here," I murmur as I head down the hallway, wondering if he'll listen. He's played the friendly thief well so far, so is this where he follows and murders me? Or will he bolt, scared I've changed my mind and

36

escape while he can? We're both skirting a tentative, precarious line, neither one willing to fully make the jump.

After checking that the living room is empty of stepbrothers, I use the bright Christmas tree lights to illuminate my path to the tree, finding two presents I know he'll make money off of. Mom FaceTimed me the other month, raving about the things she bought Dean for Christmas, and thankfully, knowing Mom, I'm very familiar with her wrapping skills. Or lack thereof, which means anything in a gift bag beneath the tree is from her because she sucks at using wrapping paper. I double check the tag, pleased with myself when I'm correct.

With the presents in hand, I carry them back to the kitchen, to Saint who's lingering in the same spot I left him.

"These are—were—gifts from Mom to my stepdad, and she told me what's inside them, so I know they'll be helpful to you. This is a chain." I hand over the smaller bag. "Worth a lot, knowing the kinds of places my mom shops at. And a new cell phone." I slide the larger bag into his hand.

He doesn't peek inside them, just stares at me, his brows lifting and scrunching together. "You're giving me these?"

I shrug. "You were going to steal from us anyway. If you are, may as well get the better of the gifts beneath the tree. If she wanted him to have these, she shouldn't have disappeared last minute. Serves her right."

Saint slowly shakes his head. "My fuck, you really are full of bad ideas. How have you survived life this long?" He breaks his stare with me to peek inside the bags, looking through the pile of tissue paper my mother not-so-artfully placed on top of the items. "Merry Christmas to me then."

"I figure you can use them better than my stepfather can. Now that you have what you've come for, I should ask you to leave."

His crooked grin sets my insides on fire. "Suddenly so polite, but you have it, Miss." Then he bends slightly in a mock bow before tucking the bags beneath his arm and re-zipping his jacket, which looks pitifully thin.

I wonder if I should steal one of Dean's heavy and expensive coats for him but also wonder if too much charity will offend the man used to stealing what he wants on his own terms.

Saint walks to the back door, opening it as a burst of winter air blasts inside. I resist from running off, my pyjamas pitiful against the cold weather. It goes to show how heated this house is compared to the outdoors, and immediately, I feel bad for the guy I'm sending out into it.

But asking him to stay is probably the worst thing I could do. Worse than anything else I've done tonight.

He spins on the step and I grasp the door's handle, shutting it halfway to keep out as much cold as I can. The overhead light flicks on with his motion, both of us giving it a considerably long look before he returns to me, his tongue sweeping his teeth.

"Can I ask for one more thing, sweet girl?" His words are frost-lined, leaving his lips in a puff of white.

"What's that?"

His gaze rakes over me for what should be the final time, landing on my chest. My nipples are hard from the icy weather, but folding my arms over my chest proves he has an effect on me so I resist.

"I want your name."

Tapering the smile that nearly slips onto my mouth, I silently tell him goodbye and good luck as I shut the door, watching him through the glass. He smirks back, his blinks slow as snow begins to fall in that instant, the million and one unique flakes landing on his shoulder, his dark hair, and his eyelashes, melting when they lower.

With a final tip of his head, he reaches for his hood and throws it over his head, backing away from the door. I watch as Saint, the stranger appearing twice in my life, disappears into the frosty night.

After a few minutes, the sensored porch lights switch off and with them, my dark adventure is over.

FIVE
SAINT

I SPEND the night inside their shed, which has a clear line of sight to the back of the house. My sweet girl lets me know precisely which room is hers when, minutes after she kicks me out, the light to the uppermost righthand room flicks on. Her figure moves through the room, but her exact actions are shielded by thin curtains I'd love to burn.

After a few more minutes, the light switches off, and she presumably goes to bed. I picture a large one with silk sheets and a puffy duvet that she's currently sliding beneath to keep her warm from the frosty night. No doubt, her bare skin is beautiful away from the harsh outdoors. I imagine her sighing as sleep steals her away from reality, her head rolling to the side, those curls spilling over the pillowcase. The blanket will slip off her shoulders, baring the tops of her chest, those breasts naturally falling to the side, her nipples begging for attention I long to give them.

It's the kind of bed, the kind of sleep, a woman like her deserves, in a place like this. A bed for people who live their lives full of greed and wealth. She'll never know what it's like to live on the street. To make passing friends wherever she goes, if only for a comfortable bed for a night here and there.

My gaze unwillingly moves from the window with the thought that

41

she's not greedy at all. She let a stranger stay in her house, fed him, hid him, and gifted valuables away. Younger, she let valued décor walk away without caring.

No, I decide, *she's not greedy at all*. She's different from everyone else.

But she's making me become so. Because for the remainder of the night, I want what I've never wanted before.

Her. To *take* her. To dirty her up and make her only valuable to me.

Before acting on those fantasies, I pick up the two gift bags and pull the tissue paper out of them, making a mental note to grab all the garbage before I go. Last thing I'd want is for it to be found months from now when spring hits and her stepdad comes in for the lawn mower, and for the missing gifts to be traced back to this night, and to her.

I want to protect her, exactly as she's done for me.

In the small bag, like she said, is a flat box. Opening it, jewellery shines back; a thick, gold men's necklace, weighing a hefty amount, making me wonder exactly how much money her mother wasted on this thing. Everything I've stolen over the years are already-owned possessions, but this is straight from the store.

I slip it into my jacket's inner pocket, wanting the treasure closest to me for safekeeping, and open the second bag. Also like she told me, the newest model of one of the most popular cell phone brands is inside. I tug off the box's lid, stroking a finger along the shiny glass. Resale of this is at least cost, but I know plenty that'll pay even more because it's the newest model that only released a month ago and they've been back-ordered due to popularity.

My sweet girl gave me a pretty damn good Christmas after all, and while I should take off now and start my path out of town, I don't. Not for the night. Instead, I bunk down with my head against the plastic shed walls and watch her window for the remainder of the night.

❄

DESPITE IT BEING THE HOLIDAYS, the kinds of people I trade with are still active on Christmas Eve, so by midday, I'm a few thousand dollars richer, courtesy of the necklace.

The phone I kept, though. It's easily worth another two grand, and yet, I couldn't sell it. Something had me wanting to hang onto it, at least for now.

I walk back toward the broken-down house I've been calling home for the past couple weeks, past the garage I sometimes get under-the-table work through. When I skip town and move onto the next one, I'll find similar work to survive off for the next few months. Nothing permanent, forever moving on, never feeling like anywhere will be right enough to call home.

For a long time, I've been fine with that. Preferable even. The three instances I've had a home to go to, a family to love me, all have given up on me, so what's the point in putting down roots? Everyone around me always digs them up anyway.

Before I realize what I'm doing, I find myself in the same ritzy neighbourhood as last night, stopping in front of my sweet girl's house. It's Christmas Eve now, so I wonder what her and her stepbrother are doing. Baking cookies and watching movies? Singing carols by the grand tree I've seen through their windows? Maybe they've gone for a snowy walk.

I wonder what she'd do if I knocked on the door, pretended to be a friend having come visited for the holidays? Would she embrace me and pretend for her stepbrother's sake that I'm not a criminal, or would she slam the door in my face, label me a stalker, and call the cops?

I *am* a fucking stalker. Never before, never until her. Not a person anyway. Houses, yes.

I shake my head of the grim thoughts because regardless of what she's doing, she's a woman too respectable for me. She deserves someone who lives in houses like those around us. A man who works at his full-time job with benefits, drives their fancy car home, and kisses her forehead before slipping into their large bed together. A man who'll treat her like a princess and not who wants to dirty her up.

I should walk away now. By New Year's, I can be far away from her, and next Christmas when I pick my mark, I'll ensure it's no one related to her. Twice is a weird twist of fate. Three would be a goddamn sign of my budding obsession.

Instead of walking away, I find myself crossing the road, pulling my hood over my face in case anyone sees me skulking around. I follow the same path I took last night so there's only one set of footprints in the fluffy snow. Thankfully, more snow is soon forecasted and will completely cover my tracks.

I slip inside the shed again, peering through to the back of the house, skimming over every window. The kitchen's lights are low, her bedroom's turned off. By my third pass, movement catches my attention in the large living room bay window, the giant tree taking up most of the space. Behind it, though, a man moves toward a woman, his arms gesturing as he talks.

I'd die to know what her and her stepbrother are talking about. I didn't like how he touched her last night. Seemed way too familiar for family, step or not, but then I figured I might not be the best judge of character, considering my lack of family and understanding of familial ties.

I stay there all day, watching the two of them move throughout the house, until finally evening falls and with it, the sun. Lights switch on upstairs, and then off, my sweet girl getting comfortable in her bed once again as she lies down, readying for what I'm sure will be a happy Christmas morning.

I slip out of the shed, knowing I should go before I find myself unable to leave her. Before an obsession kicks off, or I find a reason to intervene on her life.

I tell myself I only want another present. More cash to hold me off.

I head for the back door, jimmying the lock once again, kicking snow off my shoes with help from the bricks before entering. The kitchen is dark and déjà vu hits, but instead of going to the fridge, I quietly tread down the wide hallway until passing the living room, that damn huge tree glowing its signals of domestic happiness.

White lights wrap the fake branches, colourful and sparkly ornaments hanging from them. Tinsel drapes much of it too, strands falling onto the obnoxious number of gifts, but it gives me an idea.

I walk to the tree, knowing I could very well get the answer I crave from the gift tags, but would prefer she tell me herself. I tug a few strands of the tinsel off the tree and a bow from a wrapped gift before turning back toward the carpeted stairs.

At the top, I turn toward the right side of the house, heading for the area I know her room to be. The door across from her is also shut, the light off, and I presume it to be her stepbrother's.

Watching his door, I grasp her doorknob and twist slowly, waiting for the *crack* to allow me inside. When all remains silent from the other room, I slip inside hers and shut the door, closing it as gently as I opened it.

She makes no noise, and I wait for my eyes to start adjusting to the dark before moving toward her. She's tucked in bed, looking even more innocent than when she found me in the kitchen. The blanket dips low on her chest, one arm beneath, the other resting to her side, exactly how I've pictured her sleeping. Her head faces the window, strands of hair resting on her cheek. Her curtain is drawn, lighting up a strip of her.

I approach the bed, lowering down on one knee beside her and reach out to stroke a finger along her smooth cheek. She makes a low noise, moves slightly but doesn't change her position.

My thumb drags along her bottom lip, wondering if she tastes like sugar. It's the holidays, and sugar is almost as vital as presents for people like her kind, no? I long to test the theory for myself.

She shifts in her sleep, turning her head to the side, so I continue stroking down the column of her neck until reaching the top of her tank.

She's so fucking soft, and better wake soon because I don't think I'll be able to stop unless she demands I do.

I draw the blanket down, letting the change in temperature wake her. She shifts again, but still doesn't, so I find the patch of skin between her shirt and shorts and pet it, dragging the pad of my finger along her skin before trailing over her shorts, pressing a bit harder in the place between her thighs.

She moans, shifting her legs before tensing. I smile into the darkness. Finally, she's awake.

"What—?"

I move up the bed, placing my hand over her mouth before she can shout and ruin everything I have planned for her.

"Shh." I lower myself so her wide, fearful eyes can take me in. If she had more self-preservation, she'd be even more scared now, but instead, her gaze softens before flicking to the window. "I came in through the back door," I answer her silent question. "Will you scream if I let go of your mouth?"

She shakes her head so I slowly release her, testing her truth-telling ability. She props herself up on her elbows, staring down at me. "Saint." My name on her lips is better than any dessert they have downstairs. "What are you doing here?"

"Came back for another present." I shift to kneel at the end of her bed, pulling the blanket completely off her before reaching into my pocket and sprinkling the tinsel over her chest, amused at my gift-wrapping ability. "Merry Christmas, sweet girl. Ho, ho, ho, and all that shit." *And Happy Birthday to me.* Twenty-six opportunities to celebrate my cursed birth, and this is about to be the only time I do.

Her legs fall open, though I'm not entirely sure she realizes she's done it. Her shorts are tiny, granting me a peek of red cloth beneath. *The perfect little gift.* I want to determine if she's as sweet down there as her nickname suggests.

"I thought you left." She glances at the tinsel on her body but doesn't remove it.

I should have. "You sound hopeful." *Give me a reason to leave now before I dirty you.*

"I-I..." She trails off, biting her bottom lip before sucking in her cheeks. Even in the dark, I can spot her cheeks darkening as she blushes with the truth she refuses to admit.

"It's okay, my sweet girl. I gave you a taste of danger and that's why you were hoping I'd come to finish the job. You want to play on the wild side, and I give you that perfect, ideal opportunity, right?"

Her brows furrow, almost hurt. "No, I was worried about you."

I hum, reaching over to shift her arms until she thumps back to the bed, her head on her pillow once more. I crawl up her body, holding myself above her, one hand on either side of her body. "You're too caring for your own good. Someone's gonna hurt you one day."

"Will that someone be you?"

She's smart to ask that, but looking at her, imagining harming her in any way makes me sick. How can I hurt the person who's becoming my entire addiction? "Never."

Her lips curl up in the corners as she tentatively smiles, still too scared to let herself go to her desires. "What present have you come for?" Lust tinges her tone, her hope that *she's* to be my gift.

She'll be one of them, but there's something else I want too.

I dip my head into the curve of her neck, doing what I wanted to in the pantry yesterday, and drag my lips over her pulse, feeling it jump with my touch. She's scared or excited and I can't wait to test her restraint for both. My teeth scrape over her skin, the sudden urge to bite down and leave my mark on her becoming stronger. Maybe I will before I go, so she has something to remember me by.

For now, I nip down to the curve of her breast, and she arches her back, a low breathy gasp filling the room with sounds she'll soon likely regret.

"Me?" she incorrectly guesses.

"No." I kiss down her chest, skipping over her top as I slide farther down the bed until I'm lying between her legs. I hook fingers into her shorts and slowly tug them down, waiting for the moment she wakes up from whatever fantasy I'm fulfilling and realizes what's happening. When she kicks me out her room, screaming for the police.

Instead, she lifts her hips so I can slide them off her, leaving her in a red pair of panties. I trail my hands up her thighs until my thumbs get the sensitive skin at the top of her leg, listening for changes in her breathing.

With two fingers, I pet over her core, not stopping until I feel the area growing wet. Fuck, I hope she gives me what I really want so I can taste her—so I can reward her. So I can unwrap her.

From my pocket, I take the bow and place it above her hood.

"God, you look delicious. The prettiest little present."

She whimpers, and while I wasn't planning on touching her quite yet, not until I get what I want, I just can't fucking help myself. Not when she's not pushing me away. Not when she looks like *this*.

I dip my fingers beneath the material, stroking over the silkiest fucking thing I've ever felt. Her head falls back into the pillow, her legs to the side.

"I want your name. Don't tell me, and I'll have to stop. I'll leave and you'll never hear from me again. Tell me, and you'll be allowed to come."

SIX
HAYLEY

MY NAME. It's such a simple price for what he's offering.

What is wrong with me? Is it fucked up to have my legs spread for a man whose name I may know, but everything else about him is a mystery? Other than the fact that he's a thief who breaks into people's homes, I know nothing about Saint.

Maybe. But he's also the person I've spent the entire day thinking about. Wandering the house while trying to play nice with Bentley, who thankfully was so busy on his laptop working, I barely had to interact with him. At one point, our parents called us and the only truce we had was collectively ignoring them, being petty together.

During the day, I stared out the back window, imagining all the places a person like Saint could disappear to. Did he have a home? A family? Was he wandering the streets alone? No answer I came up with was good enough, nor was it a good enough reason to explain why I was thinking about him at all. It's like the old version of me all over, and I'm chasing the danger, seeking someone to fill in the gaps left by my parents. I've grown past that...or so I thought.

And now he's here, in my room, after breaking into the house again. Kneeling between me, while I'm half undressed, and his finger strokes my pussy, inviting me to accept more. It's his version of asking for consent without outright asking for it.

"What'll it be? Your name or...?" His hand slides out from beneath my clothing, his intent obvious.

"Hayley," I push out, not at all clinging to the thought of teasing him longer, holding out for my own well-being. "My name's Hayley."

"Hayley," he repeats in a tone like it's praise. "Pretty. Thank you."

In a swift movement, his hand slips beneath my panties again and his finger sinks deep inside me. My back bows, and I bite my hand to avoid making noises that Bentley will overhear. He strokes my insides, almost teasingly, the sensation quickly building in my core, the muscles in my thighs clenching and unclenching with each pass of his hand.

Just when I'm about to plea, Saint removes his hand and reaches for the panties. "These are in my way." I expect him to tug them down, but the *snap* draws my attention toward his cheeky grin. With a wink, he snaps the other side of the thin material and draws the material away, slipping it into his pocket.

When he hooks my thighs over his shoulder, the bow he decorated me with falls off. He's officially unwrapped me, so now he gets to play. After all, that's what happens on Christmas morning. Gifts are unwrapped, and then used.

Saint hums, his eyes flicking up my form. "If you change your mind and decide to have me arrested, just let me taste you before you do. It'd be a shame to go prison without the chance."

That's what sane people would do, but I think it's pretty obvious by now, I'm not one of them.

He slides two fingers inside me, spreading them slightly, curling against the most sensitive part of me, and right when I think the sensation can't get any better, his mouth covers me, his tongue flat against my clit. He laps at me languidly, matching the torturous pace of his fingers' thrusts.

"Fuck." I fist the blanket, pulling it up to my face because if he's only

just begun and I haven't orgasmed yet, I'll need something to muffle my scream before Bentley hears me.

"Let me hear you," he mumbles against my core before his unhurried licks continue. "Scream if you must. Maybe it'll teach that stepbrother of yours to leave you alone."

Or have him running in here, ending this. I can't even think about how Bentley would react to find this stranger in my bed.

Probably with more sense than I am.

My care for all things other than Saint disappears with his next lick. My eyes slide shut, my hand reaching for his hair. His free hand instead snaps up, grabbing my wrist before I can make full contact with his hair. He pins it to the side.

"If you're goin' to degrade yourself with me, if you want to be a stranger's whore, you have to do it properly. No touching. No control."

His licks grow into nips, teasing my clit until the response I had to his latest comment slips away into the night, and he's all I'm able to focus on. My insides clench with my building desire, my stomach clenching with the impending wave readying to sweep me away.

His fingers curl, pressing into a wicked spot inside me that covers my vision with white lights, like the ones on the tree downstairs, and I can't hold back any longer.

"Come for me, sweet girl. Hand yourself to me, Hayley."

My orgasm hits hard—harder than any in the past, but I won't focus on that fun fact—and I turn my head into the pillow to muffle my sounds as much as possible. No matter what Saint said, I don't want Bentley to hear my depravity.

He doesn't let up, even as my pussy clamps down on his fingers and wave after wave rushes through me. His licks slow, sucking everything coming from me, but his fingers continue their delicious pace.

Just when I'm finally coming down, his fingers slide from me, granting me two seconds of reprieve before he's yanking my thighs around his head and pressing his open mouth to me, his tongue sinking inside me.

"Saint."

He growls into my core, his palms clamping tighter on my thighs as he ensures I can't escape his torture. His tongue fucks me rapidly, occasionally slipping out to flick at my swollen clit before entering me once more.

He's relentless until I come again, his name on my lips, my thighs clenching his head.

With heavy pants, my thighs finally relax enough to drop to the side as Saint lowers my hips back to the bed and crawls up my body. He's fully dressed still, and his hard erection beneath his jeans brushes against my stomach.

"You taste as delicious as I imagined. Fuck, if only I could bottle you up and take you with me."

Before I can come up with a good enough response, his hand encompasses my throat to turn me to face him and he slashes his mouth across mine for our first kiss, frenzied and messy with an angry passion.

He tastes like me, and I can't help but part my lips, allowing him to kiss me deeper, harder, to imprint himself onto me in a way no man has ever managed to in the past. Hell, in a way I've never *wanted* before.

I slide my arms around his neck to keep him in position as I lift my hips and arch into him, urging him to continue, to finish what he's started.

With a sinful chuckle, he pulls away but keeps his hand on my throat, putting just enough pressure to make him impossible to ignore. "You'd be so easy to break, sweet girl. So, so easy. Letting a stranger in your bed without knowing anything about him is a risky thing."

I meet his gaze, mine challenging when I counter, "Your name is Saint. You rob people's homes because you need the money. You're transient, never in one place for long. Despite all that, you're also a good person."

"A good person." He isn't smirking like usual. "What makes you so sure?"

"You could have hurt me but you didn't."

"So you think pain is the only sign of a man's goodness?" His fingers constrict around my throat, but still not tight enough to hurt. More like he's trying to prove he's still in control. "Why would I harm you when you're living proof of why greed is a sin?"

It's a strange statement with a meaning that passes over my head, but regardless, it steals my breath, makes my mind whirl to come up with a response.

"If you're greedy, why not just take me?"

His hand sweeps down my thigh, his touch heavy on my hip. Possessive. He pulls me to him and my legs wind his waist. "Maybe I'm trying to not be too selfish. I could grow addicted to you if I let myself."

The concept of being this man's drug sounds too good, too right—even when what he said is true. This could be a horribly bad idea.

He hikes my thigh over his hip, and there's something erotic about being half-naked while he's dressed. Then he grasps my wrists in one hand and yanks them above my head, his own dropping into my neck, his taunt mumbled into the base of my throat.

"If only I grabbed Christmas lights off your tree. Bet they could be pretty useful."

I've been tied up plenty of times before, but there's something different about handing my submission to *this* man. Something I crave more than air itself.

"You'd be good for me, right? You're so innocent, you'd let me tie you up, wouldn't you? A little walk on the dark side. That's what I'd be."

"No—" He swallows my disagreement with his mouth, kissing me until I'm lightheaded, feeling as though I'm about to pass out. Doing so means this ends, and I'm starting to get the notion that's what Saint wants.

Knock, knock!

"Shit," I hiss, all but shoving Saint off me as I jerk upright, yanking my pyjama shorts back on and then the blanket over me. "Go away!" I yell at Bentley.

Saint gets to his feet, his gaze darting between the window and the door, but I urge him to the floor on the left side of my bed. Considering the door is the opposite side, he'll be well out of view.

"You okay?" Bentley's sleepy voice calls out.

"I'm fine. Just going back to sleep. Night!"

The door cracks open despite my reassurances and Bentley's head pokes through. Narrowed eyes find me in the dark, illuminated by the hallway light he switched on.

"I'm fine," I repeat, running a hand through my curls and hoping he doesn't see how frazzled I am.

Bentley paces inside, shutting my door behind him despite the fact that we're the only ones in the house—other than my secret to my left. It feels like a threat, but thankfully, he lingers in the spot, his head tilting to the side.

"You were moaning, lil' sis."

Fuck, was I really that loud? "Bad dream."

"Hm," he replies with a slow blink, obviously doubting me. "If you want help, I'm more than happy to offer my services." He takes a step forward, but I can't let him come near the bed. He'll spot Saint and I don't have much of an explanation for his presence. Or any of one, really.

I slip out of bed before he comes too close, placing myself as a guard between Saint and him. "I'm fine."

Bentley's cold gaze studies me, stopping at my chest. Following his gaze, I notice what he has: that my nipples are hard, obvious through the tank, courtesy of Saint's touching. I cross my arms, scowling.

He reaches for me, curling my hair around a finger as he murmurs, "Maybe by the end of our time together this week, you'll understand how well we'd work."

"Maybe." *Fucking delusional.* The urge to smack is hand away is strong, but it'll only irritate him further, give him more reason to react and not leave.

He smirks, dropping my curl and spinning on his heel as he turns. "Have a nice night, Hayley. You smell great, by the way. I'll dream of it."

He shuts the door behind him, giving me a chance to finally breathe. I'm turning around, ready to announce to Saint he's safe to stand, but he's already on his feet. A shadow by my window, looking like death personified as he glares daggers at the door.

"Has he ever touched you before?"

SEVEN
SAINT

FOR THE FIRST TIME EVER, I want to kill someone. Murder. Destruction. Mayhem. The entire nine yards, all so I can keep her safe. Hayley. No other name would fit my sweet girl.

She's not *mine*, but fuck if she's that asshole's. Her stepbrother acts like he wants to be a whole lot more than siblings by marriage.

She protected me for a third time. When she could have admitted the monster beside her bed, she didn't. She *hid* me because she wants me here. The fact comes with a strange sensation in my chest.

When she got out of the bed and went to him, I very carefully peeked over the mattress, watching and gritting my teeth as he played with her curls. Curls that I also shouldn't be allowed to touch, but he *definitely* shouldn't be.

I almost gave her dirty little secret up right then and there, if only for the pleasure of being able to see his expression.

He dropped numerous suggestive comments that had me ready to stab the smirk off his face, and then to cut off his hands for touching her, but I waited until he left, biding my time until she was all mine again.

When the door shuts behind him, I stand, glaring at the spot he was last standing. "Has he ever touched you before?"

Say yes. Give me a fucking reason to end his life.

Hayley approaches, unwisely nearing the man barely clinging to his sanity. She reaches for me with a shake of her head. "He enjoys making comments like that. Thinks they're amusing."

Comments. Comments are still deserving of pain.

She touches my arm, snapping me from my daze, and I lunge for her, snatching her curls in my grip and ripping her head back with a surprised gasp. My other palm pulls her closer, keeping her against me as I walk her backwards to the bed, kissing her as angry as the past five minutes have made me.

She gasps when I shove her on the bed, ripping those shorts off her again. It's a goddamn shame the interruption forced her to cover up, and I vow not to leave until her bed is soaked by her.

I stroke her pussy with two fingers before shoving them inside her, ecstatic when her back arches, her mouth opens in an O.

"Saint," she gasps, "fuck me—please."

"I am." To emphasize my words, I hammer into her harder, no longer in gentle, teasing touches. Her stepbrother's presence royally pissed me off and I have to ensure my scent is imprinted all over her, as a warning to him, before I leave.

"No—" She reaches for me, her denial ending on a breathy moan. "That's not...what I meant. And you—know it."

"Yeah, but if I do, if I allowed myself to feel you around my cock, I'll never leave. And that's not good for you."

Just saying it aloud is a reminder of the reasons I should be running away. I got her name; I got valuables; my entire job in her house has to end. Fucking her would make walking away impossible and there's no reality that'll ever exist where I can keep her.

"Please," she repeats.

"I like you begging, Hayley." I like it a whole lot. I think I could come from her breathy pants alone. "Keep it up, and maybe I'll grant you what you want."

I press harder into her, curling my fingers, but she reaches for me again, this time heading for my waist. Given how little restraint I'm clinging to, she can't touch me, but fuck if I don't want to feel her hands gripping my cock.

"Beg me again." *Convince me.*

"Saint, *please.*"

She used my name. She wins.

I pull my fingers from her to grasp her hips and flip her over, so her head is by the edge of the bed and she's staring directly up at me. Excitement lights up her eyes and she realizes exactly what my plan is.

"Unzip me."

Immediately, she obeys, unbuttoning my jeans and then pulling the little, metal zipper down. She reaches inside, freeing me from my shorts as well, and my cock hardens more than it already was in her hand.

She strokes me, her touch softer than I've ever felt before. So prim and proper, but it's not what I need. Hell, it's not what *she* needs.

I pet her cheek, stopping by her lip before dragging my thumb over it. "Here, Hayley. I want in this pretty mouth while I make you come again. And you *will* come before the night is up." As many as I can physically pull from her.

She doesn't hesitate to take me in her mouth, sucking me in past my head while tightening her lips into as small an O as she can fit around me. She pulls back, dragging her tongue over the base of my cock, paying particular attention to the sensitive skin beneath my head before sucking me as far back as she can.

"Fuck—Hayley." White spots decorate my eyes and I thrust my hips once, gaining another inch down her throat. When I look down, I nearly come from the sight alone. Her head is thrown back, my cock swelling in her throat. Unable to help myself, I reach down to stroke the column of skin. "Fuck, you look pretty with my cock down your throat. You suck so fucking good."

Her mouth clamps tighter, her tongue flicking on my underside in response.

Before I completely lose myself, I grab her hand and rest it on my upper thigh. "If you need to breathe, tap three times. Can't have you suffocating, now can we?"

She playfully taps my leg once in response.

I lean over her, pushing even farther into her as I prop a palm up on the bed beside her for balance and reach for her cunt, nudging her legs apart. They fall to the side without any other instruction and I start stroking her, dragging my two fingers through her wetness, feeling her grow more slippery.

She moans around my cock, the vibrations creating bliss like none other. I dip inside her, and then out, petting her clit. I repeat the rotation a few times until her hips angle toward me, and she becomes twitchy and unable to stay still.

"Gonna come, sweet girl? Can't let stepbrother hear you, so be sure to keep sucking." I dip my fingers in farther, urging her orgasm, eager to feel her moaning around me. "Come, Hayley. Come for me."

She does instantly, as though the command helped her along. Her cry is muffled by my cock, but she releases me still, unable to focus on the overwhelming bliss and her sucking. Her nails dig into my hip before she remembers to flatten them, keeping her hand still as her silent safe word. I don't mind her scratches though. Hell, I crave her marks. Something of hers I can take with me.

I go to pull out of her, but she grasps my waist with her free hand and sucks me down harder, lightly biting down to tell me she wants me to remain inside her. Fucking happily.

I reach for her again, lightly tapping my hand on her wet core, but with a noise, she presses her thighs together and bends them away from me before pulling her mouth away temporarily to murmur, "Too sensitive."

She takes me back down her throat, and as much as I wanted to see her come a few more times, it's a damn honour I've tapped her out. That I've given her enough pleasure.

When her teeth graze me again, I make it known I'm not in the mood for playing. Not now, when I'm so close to the edge. I reach down and grasp her hair, keeping her head at the precise angle I want. After double checking her hand is still in place on my hip if she needs to tap out, I thrust into her mouth, making her momentarily cough.

"You okay?"

She nods, so I take it as an invitation, and, keeping her hair tight in my grip, push down her throat, pulling back to the tip, and repeating. I set a pace she keeps up with, her legs falling open again.

"You take me so good, Hayley. So fucking *good*. Getting dirty by the stranger breaking into your house is one of many bad ideas you've had."

It's the sight of her pink pussy, her mouth around my length, her tongue flicking the underside of my head that drives me over the edge.

As much as I'd love to come down her throat, I pull out of her, using the grip I have on her hair to push her off me when she fights to stay latched. I stroke my cock, first reaching over to grab the pile of tinsel that's long fallen off her and tossing it back onto her chest.

I come in streams of white, landing on her chest, marking her in a primal way I've never felt with another woman. It makes the tinsel stick to her skin, my perfect dirty little Christmas gift. I can now leave her, knowing I've placed my mark of possession on her skin.

Once my breathing regulates again, I reach down to stroke through my cum, gathering a bit on my index finger before presenting it to her. She opens her mouth immediately, sucking the digit with the same effort she did my cock, cleaning me with a sparkle to her eyes.

I step back and stare down, intending to imprint this night onto my memory. Tomorrow, I vow, I'm leaving this town for good. I've gotten what I needed, so getting away from her is key. Already, it's becoming too late.

She lies, limp on her bed, a delicious, dirty mess. All done by *me*. Her head falls to the side and a sleepy smile spreads across her face, her sigh a tribute to her exhaustion.

"I'll get you something to clean up." Not sure how, considering it means lingering in the bathroom where her stepbrother could easily find me.

"Don't," she mumbles, stretching a hand toward me. "Stay."

"I can't, sweet girl." I wait until her hand drops listless to the bed beside her before helping her onto her pillow. If she won't allow me to clean her, at least I can get her comfortable. Once she's in position, I bend, brushing sweaty strands off her face before kissing her long and deep, taking the taste of her with me. "Merry Christmas, Hayley."

Thank you for making this the greatest Christmas I've ever had, and probably ever will.

I make it to the door, only stopping when she mumbles my name. Hand on the knob, I twist around. "Will you return tomorrow?"

"I'm no good for you, Hayley. Trust me. If you really knew me, you wouldn't want me in your life. Not only are we from opposite sides of the tracks, but our tracks aren't even in the same country."

Before she can respond, I slip from her bedroom, rush down the stairs, and take off into the night.

I MADE it to the edge of town before turning around and going back to her house.

I get it now. People's greed. Because I'm fucking *greedy* for her.

Before I realize what I'm doing, it's mid-afternoon on Christmas Day, and I'm knocking on her front door, as though I was an invited guest. Which, for the sake of her stepbrother, is exactly what I'll be.

The door swings open and my sweet girl fills the doorway. Her mouth slips open—a mouth I've been reliving all night—and her hands knot in her oversized green, knit sweater. She looks so cozy in it. Leggings cling to the legs I'm still recalling around my head, and adorable, fuzzy tan slippers adorn her feet.

"What—" As fast as she starts, her stepbrother appears scowling behind her, standing much too close in my opinion.

"Who are *you*?"

"Saint." I stretch my hand toward him, pretending to be someone with manners. "Hayley's boyfriend. She invited me here since it's only you two for the holidays."

"*Boyfriend,*" her stepbrother repeats, his eyes drilling into the back of her head, meanwhile Hayley's staring at me like I've grown two heads. "I didn't know you were seeing someone."

She manages to compose herself enough to turn slightly, angling herself more toward me than him, which makes me fucking thrilled. "Um, yeah, it's fairly new."

"And you didn't think to tell me?"

"We're not exactly friends, Bentley."

Ah, good, a name. *Bentley.*

Bentley, still scowling, paces away. "Wonderful...company."

"Happy to be here," I say, filling my tone with that holiday cheer I often hear in others as I step inside, my hand brushing against Hayley's. I shut the door, pressing my back to it as the house's warmth once again welcomes me.

Bentley's watching me with narrowed eyes. "It's Christmas morning. Don't you have family to be with?"

"All dead," I reply flippantly. They're dead to me, so it's close enough to the truth.

I shed my coat, tossing it toward him, and he scrambles to catch it, his gaze taking in the material obviously too poor for his tastes. I stop paying the asshole attention as I wrap my arm around Hayley's waist and tug her possessively to my side.

"What the hell are you doing here?" she hisses as we pace away from her stepbrother.

I dip my head down, dragging my nose up the column of her neck. "Making sure he knows not to touch you."

She casts me a worried look but loses her chance to make whatever comment she's about to when her stepbrother comes up behind us, a bit too close, like he's trying to be intimidating.

"I can use a drink. Then we can all sit by the tree and have a jolly ol' time." Sarcasm rings in his tone, which I reply with at an equal level.

"Sounds great, we'll wait for you."

Bentley casts me a death glare but heads for the kitchen while Hayley tugs on my hand, leading me to one of two couches framing the tree. She pulls me down beside her, whispering, "Are you fucking insane? Do you realize how many questions he'll ask that we don't have answers to?"

"Relax." I practically melt into the couch beside her, gazing around at the life I'll never have, the woman who'll never be fully mine. "I couldn't leave after seeing how he treated you. As for your worries, we'll make up the answers as we go along."

"So this is your way of protecting me?" Her brows lift into her curls, but I smooth the skin between her eyes before wrapping my hand around the back of her neck and claiming her mouth.

For all her irritation, she thaws immediately, and I want nothing more to say fuck it and take her upstairs, letting him hear how he'll never have her.

Bentley returns then, a glass in hand, almost like he ran from the kitchen and back. He coughs and she rips away from me, her lips swollen, cheeks pink. I like that. The little signs of being mine. She smooths her hair, looking anywhere but me.

He drops into the couch across from us, his glare focused on Hayley. "You didn't tell me we'd have a visitor."

"He wasn't certain he'd be able to make it," she lies in a steady voice and I squeeze her thigh before pulling her so close to me, she's practically on my lap.

Sweeping a hand by the back of her neck, I tell him, "I'll do anything for her, so of course, I made it work."

"Generous," he utters in a flat tone. "You two met at school, I assume?"

"Yes," I lie, mind scrolling for the meager bit I know about how universities function. "In the library. Went to reach for the same book at the same time. A meet-cute, really."

Hayley stiffens in my arms as her stepbrother continues to pick apart the lies. "What's your degree?"

A degree? Shit. What kinds of programs are out there that I even know of? I've never looked at a university's website because there'd be zero point in it.

"Bio-Chem," Hayley replies with a squeeze of my hand. "Same as me. It's why we were after the same textbook."

Sweet girl's an intelligent girl to be a Bio-Chem major. There's so much I don't know about her. So much I shouldn't even be allowed to wonder, but fuck if I don't want it all.

You can't. By tonight, you'll be gone from this town. This time, it's a vow I *have* to keep.

"Hanging around till the twenty-seventh with her?" he asks. "That's when her flight home is."

Only two more days. I never thought I'd be thankful for anything this asshole had to say, but knowing she'll be leaving soon is useful. It's more reason to go, because she will too eventually. Stealing from this place may have turned into stealing the very thing I couldn't ever keep, so it's a welcome reminder.

"Tonight, actually." For the first time, I tell something truthful to Bentley, but I'm looking to Hayley when I say it. "For now, I'm only here to have a nice Christmas."

EIGHT
HAYLEY

"FOR NOW, I'm just here to have a nice Christmas."

I get the sense that Saint's had very few of those throughout his life. Maybe none at all.

I still can't believe he's *here*. My thief in the night has come out of the shadows and into the stringed holiday lights, pretending to be the man he's lying to Bentley about being.

I'm practically on his lap so if he can feel my nerves, he's doing a damn good job of hiding it while he and Bentley talk. My stepbrother tosses veiled insults and doubtful questions at Saint whose lies come naturally. Too natural, and it makes me question the little I know about him.

Suddenly, this is all feeling too real. I'm finding myself wanting to take Saint away from Bentley and learn everything there is to know about him, except Saint and I can't be in that kind of relationship. Hell, we're not even in a relationship. He's my dirty, little secret and *should* be a horrible mistake.

I stare at the side of his face while he talks, wondering when the last time he interacted with others like this was. Surely, a guy on the move doesn't hang out in people's homes often.

Unless he does. Each town he stops in, he picks a girl, manipulates her into being a good fuck, robs her place, and ditches town.

Saint catches me watching him and the smile he shoots my way, the blistering stare tells me he's not lying. That *he* isn't a lie.

"Well," Bentley says gruffly, "not sure why baby sis invited you considering we're not really having a regular holiday since our parents ditched us."

"That's fine." Saint drops a kiss to my forehead. "I'm happy to be here either way."

Bentley grumbles and downs his drink. "Fuck this, I'm out to go visit a friend who's also alone today. I don't need to see some asshole violating my sister."

"Not your sister," I call out as he disappears toward the front door.

The moment we're alone, Saint drags me over his lap, my thighs bracketing his hips. "What the hell is wrong with you? I thought you were leaving."

Hurt flashes through his eyes, but before I can explain what my question meant, he replies, "I tried. Made it to the edge of town before turning around. Didn't like how he was touching you yesterday, so I'm making a point."

It might be wrong, but my heart skips a beat. He did this for me. Because he sees Bentley as a threat, even if I know he's harmless. All bark, no bite.

"The point being?"

"That you're mine. Temporarily, of course." His teeth graze my neck, enticing a shiver from me and a hungry look from him. "I also realized, despite what I said last night, I'm already damned so why should I deny myself from the only gift I actually want?"

"That being...?"

His palm presses into my back as he sits straighter, meeting me half-way. "You."

He steals my mouth in a bruising kiss, his hands tearing at my sweater, yanking it over my head. He tosses it to the side, making me shiver. His hands travel up my spine until reaching my bra. He unhooks it, drawing it away from my body.

"Saint." My eyes dart to the door. If Bentley were to come back, this isn't how I'd want him to find us.

"Relax," he whispers, knowing my precise concerns, and his hands meld with my hair. "I promise he won't see you."

He kisses me again until I'm breathless, mindless, and senseless, panting with desire. My hips move over his on their own accord until I feel his erection through his jeans and he rewards me with a groan.

One hand shifts from my hair to my hip and in a sudden, quick swoop, he's standing with my legs around his waist and walking me away from the couch. As quick we stand, he lowers to his knees, placing me on my back in front of the Christmas tree.

Saint leans back on his knees, gazing down at me. White tree lights create dots all over my skin, but he doesn't seem to care.

"Fuck, you're beautiful."

He lowers himself on top of me, kissing me sweeter than ever before. I reach for his shirt, but he draws back, pulling it over his head. It's the first time I've seen him—truly seen him—and my fuck, he's gorgeous. His muscles are defined from a life of heartache and not from a gym. Scars decorate the skin by his shoulders and I want to know how he got them. The scars, as well as the marks on his ribs.

He follows my gaze, the tips of his ears turning pink. "Not so nice to look at, eh?"

"You're beautiful," I repeat his earlier compliment. "Scars tell a story. It makes me only want to know yours."

A strange look comes over his expression before he shakes his head, and somehow, I know what he's about to say before he does. There seems to be two versions of Saint: the gentle man full of compliments and the hardened criminal, making degrading comments about himself.

"No, you don't. My story's too rough for someone as innocent as you. It doesn't have a happy ending."

"It's not over yet. You don't know what your ending will be."

He smiles sadly. "Yeah, I do, and trust me, it's not one where the criminal gets the princess."

"But I'm not—"

His palm comes down over my mouth, blocking my next words. After a moment, he slowly tugs his hand away, replacing it with his mouth, kissing me until I forget the denial I was about to say.

As he kisses me senseless, he tugs off my leggings and then my panties, until I'm completely naked beneath him. He pulls back again to look at me, cursing softly, except coming from him, the harsh word sounds like praise.

I reach for him, undoing his belt and unzipping his jeans all without breaking his gaze. I reach inside and pull out the cock that filled my mouth last night, stroking him to full length. All I could think about when he was down my throat was what he'd feel like inside me.

His eyes bore into mine like he's trying to memorize the moment. They tell a story, but it's in a language I'm not entirely familiar with.

He lets me have my fun with him, his mouth slowly falling open as his breaths grow shallower. After a moment, he rips my hand off him, growling, "Keep going and I won't get to play with you, and we can't have that." He taps my thigh, instructing, "Roll to your knees."

Lust drips from his command, and I'm more than happy to comply. In front of the tree, I get to my hands and knees, staring at the Christmas lights as his fingers slide along my clit.

"Fuck, you're already wet." He pulls his hand back for a moment, and I twist, watching him suck his finger into his mouth, pulling it out with a sweep of his tongue. Then he lowers his hand between my legs again and slides his finger back inside me, sinking deep until my gaze breaks from his and my head falls forward with a long moan.

"Don't be quiet, Hayley. Not this time. We're all alone."

Saint thrusts his finger in and out before pulling out to add a second, curling them inside me. The angle nearly shoots me off immediately, but I vow to hold on a bit longer. I don't want this to end.

As fast as I think it, the sparks inside my core build. His thumb sweeps over my clit and the combination of sensations brings my body higher and higher. My arms grow weak and I end up with my chest on the floor, my head scraping the edge of the tree skirt, my hips moving in tandem with his thrusts.

"Fuck," I cry. "Saint!"

"Sing my name, sweet girl. Treat it like a carol. Let the neighbourhood hear who you're dirtying yourself for."

Again with the self-degradation, and I want to tell him to stop it. That I know he's not that kind of person. But as fast as I'm able to get my mouth functioning, he thrusts again, harder, and I come around his hand, my cry echoing through the high-ceilinged room, my core clenching on his fingers.

Saint rewards me by finger-fucking me as long as I can physically manage before slowly pulling out of me. I turn in time to watch him studying his wet fingers in the tree's lights with a pleased smirk.

"Look how drenched you are." He puts one finger in his mouth, his draw long and slow before his eyes sparkle with mischief. "Should we see how many fingers we can fit?"

He takes my whimper as an agreement—which is exactly what it was meant to be, and when his hand lowers to my pussy again, it's with three fingers.

He's going to stretch me and it'll probably burn, but I can't find it in me to care. I'm realizing, this man can do anything to me, and I'll accept it. Accept *him*.

With three fingers, he moves slower, his other hand stroking over my spine as he makes soothing noises, sprinkled with bits of praise.

"You're doing so well."

"You're a greedy girl."

"You're beautiful, sweet girl."

Eventually, he stops stroking my back to pet my clit instead. Nothing intense; just lazy slow touches that cause my legs to shake, my head to drop onto my arms. It's a contradiction to how full my core feels and the slight burn accompanying it.

"My...fucking...god."

His thrusts slowly pick up their pace, the sounds getting wetter—more erotic. I'm mindless in my drive to come like this. To respond to his praises.

A full body shiver wracks me with my next orgasm.

NINE
SAINT

I'VE GIVEN UP PRETENDING. Pretending that she's not crack for me. That she's more addicting than the gooey Christmas cookies often baked in kitchens like the one down the hall. Eaten in sitting rooms like this one, around a tall, extravagant tree like this one.

Why should I deny myself with what I'll soon be losing?

She's not mine. Never will be. I know that, but I'll be damned if that disgusting stepbrother of hers thinks she'll be his.

I pull my fingers from her drenched pussy, taking my time in savouring each one before wrapping the same hand around my cock. It's rock hard with desire and annoyance that I didn't do this last night. I should have, could have experienced her multiple times already instead of only the one time I'm about to.

I drag my cock back and forth over her core. Her needy whimpers imprint onto my soul, her hips trying to chase my movements to push me inside her.

"I don't know how I'll ever be able to leave after this." A statement made more for her than me. "You ready?"

She flips her hair over her shoulder to face me, nodding. Desire drips from her expression and I anticipate meeting her every need. Keeping her gaze locked to mine, I push inside her. With every inch gained, her eyes roll further into the back of her head until she's no longer able to keep looking my way. Her breathing grows staggered and her head hangs low, fingers pressing into the hardwood floor by her head.

"Fuck, you take me so good, sweet girl. Your cunt knows exactly what it wants."

She says nothing, but her low moan tells me she's heard me.

I keep going until I'm fully seated inside her, hissing as her tight pussy clamps around my cock, making everything else fade away. She's so tight, it won't be long.

Her head lifts up, her arms shaking as rapture overcomes her. "Fuck—Saint. You're—" She breaks off, her back tensing.

Gently, I move, stroking my hands down her spine in a calming manner. "You okay?"

"Yes," she hisses. "You're just—fucking *thick*. I knew that...obviously. But this is—different."

I roll my hips into her, and she gasps. I grab her ass with one hand, holding her hip with the other as I move, relentless in chasing both our orgasms. Her back arches, seeking the perfect angle, so of course, I want to help. I fist her hair, wrapping the strands around my fist, and wrench her head back, arching her back and making her core tighten.

"You look so damn pretty on your knees for the common thief. You've no idea what you've done."

You ruined me. How can I hate on people's greediness when you've made me greedier than anyone?

"What have I..." Her question trails off as a moan takes her.

I slam my hips into her again, using her hair to pull her back onto my cock. In and out, my hips and grip working in tandem, playing her body for my own needs. For my greediness.

"You've given me a taste, sweet girl. How does one eat anything else after tasting something so divine?"

And my god, she is *divine.* If I don't break her by the end of this, I *have* to taste her one more time.

"They don't," she whispers, and I pretend not to have heard her. It's a daring offer from a girl as good-natured and innocent as she is. Her last day in town is in two days, and once she wakes in her own bed on the twenty-eighth, she'll understand that me leaving was my gift to her and why it was the best thing I could have ever done.

"God, you feel so fucking right." I thrust into her, keeping my movements paced and dragging out the pleasure. I feel every inch of her as I move in and out. Every little nerve jumping in response. "I like you like this. On your knees, your face lit up by the tree's lights. I get what people now mean when they talk about Christmas cheer."

"Saint—harder."

Harder? She wants *harder.* For fuck's sake, she's going to kill me.

How I can deny her such a request when I have nothing else I'm able to gift her? This is all I'll ever be able to give her. As the villain in the night, sneaking through her house, fucking the house's mistress on her hands and knees like a regular whore.

She's not a regular whore though. She's mine. All fucking *mine.*

At least for now.

Before my thoughts linger too long on that, with the grip I have in her hair and my other hand reaching out to flatten against her stomach, I straighten her onto her knees so her back is to my chest, her neck bared for the taking. I use her hair to keep her against me.

When I thrust again, it's with my face in her neck, breathing in her delicious scent. She smells faintly like sweat and me, and I hope she never washes it off, even when it's a fantastical thought that'll never come to pass. Of course, she'll shower, and once she wakes in her actual home, she'll be thankful she's gotten rid of every trace of me.

"You're too good to be down there," I growl into her skin. "I want you here, watching the tree with me like we're some sort of happy ending."

She cries out, her pussy clamping. Her eyes slide shut but with a gentle tap to her cheek, I wake her up.

"Eyes open. I want you here with me."

"As if there'd be anywhere else," she whispers, locking her eyes onto the tree.

My thrusts speed up, the compelling urge to come so overwhelming. It won't be long now, but damn, I want it to be. I want to drag this out for as long as I can. All night ideally. So long as I don't have to let her go.

"Please tell me you're on birth control."

"Yes, and I'm safe."

"Thank fuck."

I thrust harder, and when I come, it's with my hand on her hip and the other on her throat, my teeth in her neck, and my heart in her hand. I come with a growl, an imprint to her insides for every fucker she allows inside her in the future.

My next statement—my vow—I say into her neck, stamping it there so anyone she allows around her will feel it for themselves.

"If *anyone*, your stepbrother or otherwise, even *considers* harming you, I'll hunt them the fuck down, Hayley. I don't care if I have to travel from one end of the country to you, I'll always protect you. Even though I can't keep you, you're mine now, and I protect what little I can call mine."

Another woman would have run away from me right then and there, *finally* understanding the dangers in having a criminal in her life. Someone who doesn't attend a fancy school, or have major career aspirations like she does. But not Hayley.

She twists in my arms and my cock slips out of her. She stares at me, her mouth parting to speak, but anything she'll say will make it worse, so I kiss her instead. Closed mouth, and sweeter than I'm usually capable while my hands trail up her sides, over her breasts, and back down to her pussy, dripping with my cum.

Then I hold her. Hold her, enjoy her.

After a couple minutes, Hayley pulls out of my arms and settles beside me, her back to my chest. She's staring past the tree and out the window, where snow is beginning to fall again. A picture-perfect holiday —and the best birthday celebration I've ever gotten. The only one, really.

"Why do you move around so much?" she asks suddenly. "Could you not stay in one place for a while?"

"Not with the stealing. I always worry it'll get traced back to me."

"Don't steal," she says like it's so simple. She doesn't understand how stealing things provides an instant payday greater than any job I'd manage to get.

I ignore that comment and return to her other one. "Habit, I think. I was kicked out of every foster home I've ever been in, and settling in one place became a strange concept. No town I stopped in ever felt right enough to make it permanent so I kept going. *Keep* going. I guess I'm looking for somewhere suitable enough to call home but haven't found it yet."

"If you do find it, would you stop moving around?" Her question has a strange edge to it.

"I'll never find it, so it's a pointless question." My answer is also a lie because I've already found it.

Hayley turns slightly, settling against my chest, and I wrap my arm around her back, almost cradling her. She pets my chest, staring at her hand instead of me. "That's really sad, Saint. I'm sorry for your childhood."

I don't respond. Can't respond. Just stare mutely at the tree and pretend this little woman isn't breaking me piece by piece.

After a moment, she follows my gaze and her eyes lock on the presents beneath the tree. When her head rolls back to look at me upside down, I suspect her question before she asks it. "What'd you do with the ones I gave you?"

"Pawned the jewellery for cash. Kept the phone."

"Oh? Why?"

"Not sure." It's not something I really want to dissect right now either. My gaze lands on the nearest present, with a tag marked *From Dean*. Presumably her stepfather.

She notices me watching but incorrectly guesses what's in my head. "You can take it if you'd like. It's a gift to my mom. Not like she needs more junk."

If I was smart, I'd take her up on her offer. Hell, if I was really smart, I'd send her on her way to get cleaned up and clear everything out from beneath the tree. But I'd already gotten what I came for, and taking anything more right after fucking her feels...wrong. I don't have many morals but cheapening sex with the only woman to make my heart skip a beat isn't how I want this to end.

"It's fine. Is Dean your stepdad?" She nods, and I add, "Do you like him?"

"He's alright," she replies with a shrug against my chest. "He's nice, but I'm tired of my mom hopping between husbands."

Her comment reminds me of our first meeting four years ago, when her parents followed her out of the house. I always wondered what caused the drama, but was also very grateful for the reason. Either way, back then, they were still together, which means Hayley's had plenty of family turmoil in the past few years.

"What happened between your parents?"

"Mom cheated on him with the man who later became my first stepfather. The day I met you, the fight you saw, it was because a text on Mom's phone revealed what she'd been doing behind my dad's back. It led into a massive argument—rightly so...but all I wanted was for them to stop. To have a Christmas full of cheer and all that. They wouldn't stop yelling so I took off." She smirks up at me. "I didn't have great emotional regulation back then. Anyway, by New Year's, a divorce settlement was signed. By the following June, Mom remarried, and Dad took off to tour the world in a midlife crisis or something. That marriage lasted a year before Mom decided he wasn't financially well-off enough, and then got with Dean." She snorts, shaking her head. "And when I say stable, I mean uber rich." She waves her hand to the room. "It's a bit much, isn't it? Mom is, and yes I'll say this about my own mother, a gold-digger."

So much about Hayley's personality just came out within that speech. So much a part of me knew from night one, but didn't totally understand it either. "That isn't who you are."

"My goal is to be stable enough in my career to afford life because unfortunately, money is how the world turns. Beyond that, I don't really care. I don't want to be like her."

"Chasing money?"

She sighs. "That...and everything else. She cheated on Dad, and I never forgave her for ruining our family. I haven't had a good Christmas since I was seventeen. Honestly, there's so much, but I'd be here all night."

I could easily listen to her recount everything of her childhood to me, all night long. Hell, I want it—to know everything there is about her. But I respect why she doesn't want to go down that path.

I consider her words. How, for a long time, my wish was to have a family, but Hayley, in that single story, has proved having a home like the one we're in, a family like what she has, isn't always the happy ending we like to think it is. People have secrets and shit backgrounds.

"This has been the best Christmas in a long time," she murmurs suddenly, and my chest warms.

"I'm glad, Hayley." I rub a palm down her arm, revelling in being able to touch her so freely. "For me too." It's been my *only* good holiday. The only birthday I've been content to be alive for. "If you could wish for anything in the world, what would it be?"

She's silent for a while, almost to the point I think she's ignoring me. Finally, her answer comes in the quietest voice I've heard from her yet. "I don't know."

A part of me is thrilled to hear her say that
Another part of me is fucking terrified.
I need to get out of here before I take one more item from this house.
Her.

TEN
HAYLEY

SAINT GETS STRANGELY quiet after I finish talking, his stare locked on the tree instead of me. I feel him pulling away and try to remind myself this is positive because my stranger in the night can't be permanent. Not when I'm returning to school in two days and he's going...somewhere.

"Even though I can't keep you, you're mine now, and I protect what little I can call mine."

As messed-up as it may be, I have become his in the past twenty-four hours. A part of me will always belong to my dark thief. He was the Christmas miracle I didn't realize I was waiting on.

"If anyone, your stepbrother or otherwise, even considers harming you, I'll hunt them the fuck down, Hayley. I don't care if I have to travel from one end of the country to you, I'll always protect you. Even though I can't keep you, you're mine now, and I protect what little I can call mine."

Those aren't words from someone who doesn't care.

Abruptly, Saint stands, pulling on his jeans and then his shirt before silently walking away from me. Tears prick my eyes, but I bite my tongue and gather my clothes, redressing in case Bentley returns from wherever he disappeared to. I won't cry yet. Won't allow myself to *feel* any of this.

Saint returns after a couple of minutes to find me partially dressed and staring glumly at the tree, the memory of what we did in front of it replaying in my head. This really has been the best Christmas I've had in a long time, and while I'm sure a psychologist would love nothing more than to pick that tidbit apart—that my happiest holiday is with a criminal over my family—it doesn't make it any less the truth.

He scans me once, frowns, and then comes for me, one arm beneath my legs, the other around my back and he lifts me, carrying me from the living room. Silently and swiftly, he carries me up the stairs, but instead of going to my bedroom, he stops at the first door in the hallway: the bathroom. The light's already on, and soapy water fills the tub.

He prepared a bath for me.

While I'm finding the words, Saint peels off what little clothing I managed to put back on and lowers me into the tub. The water is hot, but doesn't burn, and immediately muscles I hadn't realized were tense unknot. My head falls back against the wall while my eyes fight to stay open.

Saint takes a seat on the edge of the tub and walks his fingers from my chest to my neck. He bends and presses a kiss to my lips, and then my forehead, sighing before pulling away, his dark eyes a shadow of themselves.

"This is it, isn't it?"

He nods, pressing his lips together. "I didn't expect this job to go anything like how it had, but I have no regrets. Anyway, you're going back to school soon and I don't like to hang around one place too long."

Suddenly, being naked around him feels too much, and thankful for the bubbles he's filled the tub with, I pull them close to me, shielding myself from his gaze.

He watches me, frowning but not stopping me. "I'm sorry for ruining your holiday."

"You didn't."

His next smile doesn't meet his eyes, like he doesn't believe me.

"You're still too innocent. Don't feed the next strange man who tries to rob from you."

Only you.

He stands, moving to the doorway. "Goodbye, my sweet girl. Remember what I said."

With that, he's gone.

Again.

A few minutes later, I hear the front door shut.

I wonder what else he took from beneath the tree.

And decide I don't care.

IT'S hours later when I finally get out of the bath, long after the water has cooled and when I realize it's now nine at night, and Bentley could be back soon. I dry off and head to my room, dressing in the first pyjamas I find in my suitcase and then sliding into bed, doing my hardest not to look out the window and wonder where Saint is. No doubt, off on his adventures, getting far away from here. At the last second, I part the curtains, needing to feel that much closer to him.

I try not to let it hurt. Try not to cry on Christmas. Try not to feel anything about the stranger who snuck into this house and into my life and gave me a taste of what I'd been missing. How he saw me in ways few others have, even after only a day.

The door thumps from way down below and I turn over to face the window in case Bentley decides to check if I'm awake or not. Wherever he's been and whatever he has to say about my surprise boyfriend can shove it.

Heavy, threatening steps tread up the stairs, and I think about exactly how heavy he's walking for me to hear them over the staircase's carpet and behind my shut door. They approach my door before disappearing into the one across, and with a sigh, I shut my eyes, thankful I won't have to deal with him tonight. Or for much longer. One more day and then I'll be heading home and he can return to the fancy condo he crawled out of.

I'm dozing off to the thoughts of Christmas lights and a particular wicked boy in the nighttime when my door abruptly slams open, the knob hitting the wall hard enough it probably left a dent.

A light switches on, blinding me, and I'm barely upright, a shout of, "What the *fuck*, Bentley?" scarcely out of my mouth before he's beside me, bearing down, his arms on either side of my body.

I recline on the bed to get away from him, realizing my mistake a second too late because I'm exactly where he wants me. He crowds me even more, ensuring I have no way of escaping.

"Who the fuck is he really?" The scent of stale beer wafts off him, his crazed eyes narrowed. He staggers slightly, like even the grip he has on my sheets isn't enough to stabilize him. "He's not your boyfriend, so don't give me that bullshit."

"Bentley!" I push into his chest, but he doesn't budge. "Get the hell off me, you maniac!"

"Who. Is. He?" His teeth bare beneath his curled lip.

"Believe me or don't, but it's none of your business either way."

It must have been the wrong thing to say because he rips the blanket off me, but I don't give him the chance to do anything before kicking a leg into him and rolling to the other side of the bed. Another mistake, since now I'm farther from the door. He might have strength and size on his side, but he's wasted and unfocused, so hopefully that works to my benefit.

I run around the bed only for him to move so much quicker than expected. His arm bands around my waist, shoving me backwards.

"Bentley! What the fuck is wrong with—"

Smack!

The sting registers on my cheek seconds before my back hits the window, the cold glass would otherwise be a bother if it wasn't for the situation. He lunges at me, one hand clamping around my neck, squeezing tightly.

"You lied to me tonight, you little whore."

I tip my chin forward, trying to give him the least space as possible while my hands claw at his arm, seeking freedom. His fingers pinch my throat, cutting off my airways, and my hits are doing little to distract him.

"Bentley...let me—"

He snarls, his eyes narrowing while his other hand slips beneath the edge of my tank. "I'd like to see what all the fuss is about first."

My heart hammers as sweat breaks out on my brow and fear consumes me, threatening to lock my muscles. I can't fight him, not completely, not like this. He's too strong and his grip is making my vision blurry, my blood rushing through my ears until it's all I can hear. My focus remains on the meager sucks of breath I'm able to take.

"S-stop...Let...go..."

Then he does. He's ripped off me with a loud bang. A crash of fury. Of fists.

By a man who says things like, *"I protect what little I can call mine."*

ELEVEN
SAINT

EVEN WHEN I walk away from her after preparing her bath, I don't leave. Why? Because I'm a fucking moron who instead lingers outside her house, watching and waiting for the bathroom light to turn off and for hers to switch on. That's when I'll leave for good, I decide. When I see she's tucked into bed on this Christmas night, visions of sugarplums visiting her dreams rather than me.

When I do see her, it's an outline hidden behind that fucking curtain I still want to burn. The delicate material reminds me of the kind of woman she is, and the kind of man I'm not. I'll never be like the people she goes to school with; the future businessmen and lawyers, doctors and architects who'll make the world a better place. They're everything I'm not and will never be.

After a few minutes, the light flicks off, but she draws the curtains open. She could very well be only letting the moonlight into her room, but I let myself fantasize that I have something to do with it.

So I don't leave. Not yet. Soon though, I will.

More minutes pass, my eyes growing heavy when her light abruptly switches on again. I straighten from my slouch, heart beating a bit faster. Then I see her through the sliver she's granted me by parting the curtain. She shoots up in bed, her attention toward her door and that's when I realize something is wrong. Very, very wrong.

A figure moves into view, leaning over her. Her stepbrother. She shoves him away, but he pushes her down, and that's all I wait around to watch before I'm cutting through the yard and toward the back door.

Now, having picked this lock a few different times, the door opens quickly and I rush through the house, passing the living room that now holds better memories for me than any other house I've been inside or lived in, and up the stairs, taking them two at a time.

I don't stop, throwing her door open, reading the scene for only a second before reacting.

She's pinned to the window, his hand tight on her throat. Her eyes flutter shut, even while she continues trying to push him off her, her nails imbedded into his wrist and she doesn't see me burst in.

He does, though. He glances over his shoulder, his mouth parting. I don't give him a chance to talk before ripping him off her. Hayley moves quickly, ducking to the side of the room and I push him against the window, in the place he had her pinned hard enough the window cracks, just a tiny spider one.

He was trying to hurt her, so I'll hurt him. It's as simple as that.

I lunge at him, landing throwing fist after fist into his face. Bentley might be around my size, but his muscles are manufactured with his expensive gym membership. The man doesn't know genuine work. To live on the streets and fight for what you want, what you own. It's do or die out there, and more than once I've gotten into scraps to protect food, clothing, or other critical items.

And Hayley is *mine*. On the streets or in this house, against a gang or against one asshole stepbrother, I'll always fucking protect her.

After my fourth punch, he seemingly wakes long enough to manage to duck the next oncoming one and to dive toward me instead. He staggers, clumsy and injured, alcohol wafting from him.

But I'm quicker. I pause for a moment, crouched, letting him approach before springing up and jamming my shoulder into his stomach, shoving him back to the window.

Everything happens at once then.

That spider crack in the window crumbles beneath the force I shove Bentley's body into it, shattering the glass. It falls to the ground below.

And Bentley alongside with it.

"No!" Hayley yells, pushing away from where she was out of the way. She reaches the window and sticks her head outside. "Shit!"

I'm stuck, almost numb, as I watch the scene unfold. No way he'd survive a fall from this height, snow or otherwise. If he had, it's likely he won't be awake anytime soon. It's quite possible I accidentally killed him.

She turns away from the window, her face whiter than ever—all except for the red staining her skin. Her cheek for one, and the shadows surrounding her neck from where he was gripping her.

Fuck, he better be dead or I'll go down there and finish the job myself.

I want to go to her, hold her, tell her he'll never touch her again, but I'm still numb, watching as she paces by me, wringing her hands together.

"I-I have to go check on him."

She heads for the door and I turn to follow, only for her palm to quickly come between us. Of course, she doesn't want me anywhere near her. I'm a monster who just ruined someone's life, dead or otherwise.

"Stay. One way or the other, I'll have to call 9-1-1. If there's two sets of footprints in the snow back there, they'll question it."

Fuck. Me. Even now, after everything...she's protecting me by limiting the evidence the police would find here.

My throat stops working entirely so I merely watch her dash off before heading for the window, eyes skimming the surrounding houses. Everyone's lights are off and the window breakage didn't make much noise, and no one's come running in the past few minutes so at least there's no witnesses.

Hayley's now outside and she slowly treads toward her stepbrother's body. His face is marked with gashes from my punches, but it's the angle of his neck suggesting his injuries are beyond a few cuts and bruises.

Hayley approaches him, and I hate it. I don't want her anywhere near him, especially if he's dead. She crouches by his side and reaches a finger toward his neck, checking for a pulse.

It's the longest two seconds of my life, but when she looks up at me, my suspicions are confirmed even before the slow shake of her head.

Dead.

This should be the moment guilt creeps in, but it never comes. Sometimes, it's kill or be killed, and after living on the streets, things like other people's lives matter less. It's me or them, and I'll always choose myself. In this case, I chose *her*.

Hayley backs away from him and returns inside the house. I listen for her steps coming up the stairs and back toward her room, wondering at what point she'll realize what I've done, how big of a monster I am, and she won't look at me how she had in the bath. She'll understand what taking me in like a stray dog has done to her life.

Her eyes are downcast as she enters and I wait for her to make the first move. To demand I stay so she can have me arrested. If I go to jail, it'll be worth it knowing he'll never harm her again.

She crosses the room, every step toward me one more piece of my sanity she's stealing for herself. She breathes in and out through parted lips once, twice, before blinking, her gaze finding me again. Her hand cups mine, the one I hit him with, the fucker's blood staining her palm.

It's all I can focus on. The wrongness of it.

"Thank you for saving me."

She's not cowering. She's *thanking* me. This fucking girl...Before I'm not allowed to anymore, I cup her face in both hands, remembering this look. The look before she comprehends what it means to have a dead body in her backyard.

"I told you, I'll protect you. Always. Against anybody." My fingers stroke over the red mark on her cheek, thumbs brushing the dark shadows blooming on her neck, the desire to hit him becoming so overwhelming once again. "He hit you. Strangled you. Are you okay?"

She nods shakily, rubbing her hands up my arms. "I-I should call the police before neighbours notice him back there."

"I'm not sorry," I tell her. "He was hurting you."

Her eyes flutter shut for a brief second. "Is it wrong to say I'm kinda happy he's dead? Does that make me a bad person? I never thought I'd want anyone dead, but he—"

I don't think. Just act. Just *react*.

Because my sweet girl is so fucking perfect.

I snap, and before I fully realize what I'm doing, I have her pants yanked down, mine undone. A few strokes for us both and I have her seated on my cock, her legs around my waist, her arms draped over my shoulders as I thrust her into the wall.

I murdered someone.

I protected her.

I've claimed *this is it* too many times with this girl, but this time, it's the truth. I have to get the fuck away from here—far away.

Until then, while I have her for this moment, before I risk her changing her mind and going from thrilled to heartbreak and hating me, I fuck myself into her.

It's quick and quiet, only the sound of my thrusts and her little moans filling the room. I duck my head to bite her nipple through her shirt and she rewards me with nails scraping my shoulder.

"You're safe," I whisper to her between thrusts. "He'll never go near you again. No one will ever hurt you, sweet girl. Not if they want to live."

Her pussy clamps down on me, her head tossed back into the wall as she cries out her orgasm. I drink up every sound, every breath, as I too thrust a final time inside her, lingering long after we both come down, not wanting the moment to end.

Too soon, her eyes flick toward the broken window and widen, the spell officially failing. *This is it. She'll hate me. Her previous comments mean nothing—*

"Y-you have to get out of here." She pushes against my shoulder until I unwillingly lower her to her feet. "I-I'll claim it was self-defence. I can't be charged for that. I think. Not with the marks on my neck."

I study the broken window she's about to claim she's broken when pushing out of it. The cops will never believe this tiny girl managed that. I grab her as she tries to rush by me, bringing her fist up to my face, stroking the back of her silky, soft skin.

"Hayley, they won't believe you."

Anguished eyes turn on me, and it's an immediate punch to the gut. Harder than any I'd given the body on the ground. "I don't care," she says in a determined growl. "I won't see you go to prison because that's exactly what'll happen. I was fighting for my life and got a burst of adrenaline. You hear about this all the time. They'll have no other evidence to go off of."

I'd go to prison without a paid fancy lawyer to back me up, while her stepfather would pull out every stop for his son. It's a fact I'm almost certain of. I'd be a statistic. Foster kid ended up on the streets, surviving, only to end up locked up. All for her. I'd like to say in ten years I'd regret it, but I wouldn't. Not if it means he'll never look at her again.

"You protected me," she goes on. "It's my turn now."

My fucking god, the more she speaks, the more winded I grow.

Still holding her hand, I mentally scroll through every option we have —and there aren't many. Any, really.

I may have protected her from him, but she's now trying to protect me from the law. In order not to be charged with homicide in the case of self-defence, the cops will need to believe she had more reason to defend other than him sneaking into her room. Hopefully the marks on her body will be proof enough, but if they're not, it'll be her freedom on the line and I can't stomach the thought. Not when she has a promising future ahead of her and I don't.

No one's ever protected me. No one's ever saved me. No one's ever wanted to.

But she has. In every fucking sense of the word, she's saved me...and there's nothing I can ever repay her with.

"This will work," she insists, sensing my turbulent debate. "It'll be up to the courts to decide if they want to prosecute, but it was my life or his. They'll take my side."

"You're not selling this concept very well."

Hayley reaches for my face. *"Please.* You need to leave right now and I won't breathe a word to anyone, I swear."

I turn away, unable to look at the monster I've created. This innocent girl went from letting a thief eat her food and openly steal from her to participating in a murder cover-up. Fuck, I'm so bad for her, even if she's becoming everything I want.

"I'll go now. Wait five minutes and call the police. Then your parents."

I'll go...but not far. Not until I know she won't be taking the fall. The second I see her imprisoned, I'll hand myself over.

I want to kiss her one more time. Kiss her while my cum still drips from her pussy, but I've ruined her life enough.

Goodbye, my sweet girl.

I vanish into the night, disappearing from the house that was supposed to be a simple robbery.

In the end, its stolen more from me.

Hayley robbed me of everything I was and made me want something else, to be someone new.

But I can't be greedy with her.

Not anymore.

TWELVE
HAYLEY

THE HOURS FOLLOWING the accidental murder are a whirlwind of emotion. Once Saint escaped, I truly broke down, which made my call to the police more believable. Then I called Mom, feeling horrendous when having to tell Dean about his son's death over the phone. They hopped on the first available flight and will be home later today.

The police and ambulance show up, and everyone seems to accept the story I feed them, which is mostly the truth, sans Saint. That Bentley arrived home drunk and started attacking me. I fought back, using every bit of strength I mustered. At one point in the struggle, I pushed him at the window, which happened to be harder than I believed, and Bentley crashed through. I ran outside to check on him, and then called 9-1-1.

The coroner, who followed a short while later, confirmed he was dead on contact with the ground, the snow not quite enough to cushion him. The medics confirmed the prints on my neck, the mark on my cheek, and the blood on my hands all coming from the fight, which left the police to believe me, though I still had to go downtown for this to all get sorted.

When I arrive, a lawyer is already waiting for me, courtesy of Mom.

The lawyer tells me to remain silent on anything else, that this was purely self-defence, and that charges should be avoidable. After a long conversation with the police chief, she returns to tell me they're not pressing charges since they feel if I didn't fight, it'd be me in the morgue instead, and the fall was a consequence of the fight.

I wait around the station for Mom and Dean. The second they enter, Dean is a complete wreck on the floor, gaining a large audience. I step around Mom, who isn't comforting her husband beyond her fake tears, to apologize. He lost his son, even if that son was a piece of shit.

"I'm really sorry," I say. How else do I address the fact I'm behind his son's murder?

Dean looks up long enough to scan my face and neck. His expression pinches before he murmurs, "So am I. I-I didn't realize he'd be capable... I'm sorry you did what you felt you needed to."

The conversation doesn't end the storm inside me, the wonder of how much he truly hates me now. How much he's blaming me. How we'll all go on from this.

I leave him when the police officers who answered my 9-1-1 call go to talk to him and return to Mom's side, who merely fusses with my neck. "Makeup will cover that up."

Jerking my face away, I reply with a glare. After everything that's happened, she's still only focused on outward appearances.

Once the police discharge me to go home, she trails me out, insisting she'll drive me home rather than stay with Dean. I assume, she's avoiding. Her marriage just got more real, and if I know Mom, she'll be running soon.

"I'm tired," is all I say when we get home. I enter the front door and head to the staircase without looking toward the tree, or into the bathroom. Anywhere that reminds me of *him*. I hope he's gone. Far away and safe, robbing other homes.

Thankfully, Mom doesn't follow and I shut my door with a heavy sigh. The room is still chilly from the broken window but warming with assistance from the house's high temperature settings. After the forensics team got what they needed from my window, they were nice enough to tape up plastic and keep the winter weather from coming inside.

I head straight for the bed, driven by pure longing and curiosity. Before the police took me to the station, they cleared out of my room so I could change out of pyjamas and into clothing more weather appropriate. In their absence, I wrote a note and hid it beneath my pillow, feeling the intended owner would return for it.

When I lift my pillow, holding my breath, the note is gone. The scrap of paper with only my name and number. Which means, amidst the crime scene, the police being in and out, he risked returning.

In its place is something else. Something explaining his reason for coming back.

A pink, leather-bound journal with a note on top.

SO YOU CAN WRITE DOWN ALL YOUR WISHES AND FIGURE OUT WHAT IT IS THAT YOU WANT.

—S.

It's not the journal that brings tears to my eyes, or even the note left behind, or the fact he risked coming here to deliver it. It's that my thief in the night who steals from houses, *gave* something to another person.

To *me*.

I hug the journal to my chest and wander toward the window, gazing at the dulled evening sun through the thick sheet of plastic, wondering where he is. Hoping he's safe.

Missing him.

THE TWENTY-SEVENTH FINALLY COMES, but leaving isn't without hesitation. When I showed up here the day before Christmas Eve, I assumed I'd be bored until my flight home. Now that it's come, I stare longingly at the room again, recalling when Saint woke me up before licking between my legs. Or when I was upside down, sucking him down my throat. Or everything else that happened here.

Downstairs, it's more of the same feelings. The tree has become a place of every sin possible and I feel my cheeks heating as I turn away. Mom and Dean haven't noticed the missing gifts, but then again, they've hardly been around. Mom's been in and out, while Dean spent the past day at his brother's house, who lives in town, working through his grief.

The kitchen is where I nearly broke down. It's where it all started.

Mom meets me outside after loading my suitcase into her car, twirling the keys with impatience. The moment I get in the passenger seat, she explodes, like she was clinging to whatever she has to say until able to let it out.

"Dean served me divorce papers. *Apparently*, he thinks it's not right for two people to remain married when one of their kids killed the other."

She says it so offhandedly, like a man's life wasn't the price. Sure, he was a piece of shit, but still her stepson. It might be ironic, considering my role in the cover-up, but at least I pretended for Dean's sake. Understood that no matter the person Bentley was to me, he was a son loved by his father. At least I had *compassion*, but Mom acts like the entire thing is an inconvenience.

"What?" she demands, spotting my glare.

"So you blame me?"

She doesn't reply right away, but her lips purse, probably debating the answer herself. After a few moments, she still doesn't reply but launches into a whole spiel about a new dating app she's heard good things about.

Great. Another stepdad in the near future.

She rambles on and on the entire drive and I let her, tuning her out as I imagine where Saint's gone off to. How many towns has he managed to get through in the passing days. Where his destination will be. Where the next house he'll rob will be.

At the airport, I give her a one-armed hug, which she barely returns. "Do better, Mom," I mutter at her before turning away.

The check-in line is long but goes quickly.

Security is shockingly easy and painless.

I find my gate quickly, thankful it's near the bathrooms for those last-minute trips. I claim a seat by the window to watch them load the plane. I wonder if Saint has ever been on a plane, but guess he hasn't, based on his story.

I wonder a lot about him.

While pretending he didn't steal the most important thing from me. My heart.

EPILOGUE

SAINT

One and a Half Months Later

MY INNOCENT, sweet girl left me a note when I returned to her room. I waited until all the cops cleared out before sneaking inside, using the shadows of the moon to get inside and leave the gift I spent hours that day picking out.

It's the only thing I'd ever gifted to another person, and the only one I'd ever. That much I already knew.

In the very place I left it was an unaddressed note, but I knew it was for me.

Hayley Ellison.

With her phone number scribbled on the bottom.

I tucked the paper away, hoping I'd get the chance to use it one day, when I returned to stake out the police station, holding my breath until Hayley exited the building with her mother. She wasn't imprisoned, so it was with a final longing look, I disappeared for good, her contact information now the most valuable thing I've ever gotten.

After two weeks of pretending she didn't consume my every thought, I looked her up. With her last name and the help of free computer usage at a public library, she was too easy to find. Apparently, she's one of those people who posts so much of her life online.

If I wasn't already obsessed, I became so then. For hours, I poured over every detail of her that I dug up. Old pictures on social media of her friends at high school parties and sporting events. More recent photos of her apartment and of the landscapes surrounding it. Landscapes with a location marked, making it all too easy to travel to.

Hayley once asked me if I'd ever find a place to remain in for good.

Now I have. Settled into a real job at a factory and am renting an apartment that isn't run-down and everything. Got the brand-new stolen phone activated and imputed her number into it, the only one other than my new boss's number that's listed in the contacts app.

For the month since arriving, I've stalked her from afar. At first, holding back to remain out of her life before intruding where I didn't belong. Now that the holidays passed, and our time together, she's free to pretend what happened didn't.

Then one day, I was inside the university's library, watching her study at a table from my place hidden behind shelves, and she pulled out the journal, and with it, signed herself to me in every other way she had yet to.

So now, I'm on the rickety metal balcony attached to her apartment after using the others around hers to climb to this point. The lock keeping her door shut is weak, and exactly as the clock strikes midnight on February fourteenth, Valentine's Day, I break inside her apartment, tucking the package of chocolate hearts beneath my arm.

The place smells like her. Sweet and addicting, like sugar cookies on Christmas morning—a scent I'm only familiar with from sneaking into homes after they've been baked, but also a scent I vow to recreate with her next Christmas. I pace through the living room, past the small couch and moderate-sized TV, stepping over stacks of textbooks I've seen her lugging throughout campus, and toward the bedroom.

Her door is cracked a couple inches and I take that as an invite, slipping inside and keeping my steps quiet while crossing the room. Like the room in her stepfather's place—ex-stepdad now, I suppose, since I saw the reports of their divorce online when the news outlets asked for an interview on the one-month anniversary of his son's death—her bed is in line with the window, the curtain drawn. The streetlights beyond the window light my path to her side.

She's sleeping facing it, her expression calm and peaceful. Curls fall over her forehead and I brush them away from her face, letting my fingers linger on her skin before dipping to stroke her lips, craving the taste of them. It's been entirely too long, and a length of time I'll never allow to pass again.

I continue touching her, tugging the blanket down as I bare more of her body, exactly like I did on Christmas Eve. Goosebumps sprout over her arms, her thighs, but I continue, dipping low to trail my lips down the same path.

She mumbles, rolling over in her sleep, which only makes it all the better. With a smile, I trace over the front of her tank, watching her nipples bud. I follow the path to the patch of skin above her hip, and still, she doesn't wake.

My sweet girl's ready for me. She's not wearing pants, like she hoped I'd eventually come for her. I'm too greedy to wait—a notion I now completely and utterly embrace—and slot myself between her thighs. After a final peek at her face, I draw her panties to the side and cover her core with my mouth.

She jolts awake, her legs kicking naturally at the intrusion, but with a heavy hand on each one, I keep her still and climb up her body, letting her panicked, sleepy state process the sight of me.

After three blinks, her limbs go limp. She dabs her tongue against her bottom lip and my cock jumps to life.

"S-Saint?"

"Yeah, sweet girl. I'm here. I couldn't stay away."

Her eyes dart to her window and back. "How'd you get in?"

"Do you really want me to answer that?"

"You never contacted me. I hoped you'd borrow a phone or something. Call me." Red tinges her cheeks, reminding me of the first night with her. "I mean, I guess, you were busy roaming cities." Her brows dip with that last comment, gaze going to another place. "How'd you find me?"

"You post a lot on social media," I answer her last question before sliding the cell from my pocket.

Her gaze lights up as comprehension settles. "You kept it?"

"Somehow, I knew I'd need it one day. I decided to skip the texting and come myself. I've missed you, Hayley. Once I figured out which city you live in, I booked a flight here. Got settled into a place. Got a job—a legal one. Figured I'd stick around for a bit."

"A bit" being as long as Hayley is here too, and I know she understands the meaning behind my statement.

"How long have you been here?"

"A month."

More realization dawns. "You've been stalking me."

"Yep," I answer, crawling farther up the bed as this conversation, while necessary, grows tiresome. "I wanted to see you in your life. I wanted to ensure you were still mine, that there wasn't any assholes hovering around what I've claimed. Hayley, before you, I *despised* the concept of greed. Probably 'cause I never got the chance to experience it for myself. And Christmas is the worst time of year for people's greediness. Kids demanding one present after the next. Adults wanting the latest tech to replace what they only got last year. Meanwhile, December twenty-fifth has always been a shitty day for me. It's my birthday, and no day before meeting you has ever been truly worth living."

Her mouth slips open. "You mean, this whole time, it was your *birthday* too? You never said anything!"

"Didn't have to. My wishes already came true." I give her a meaningful look before finishing my story. "Christmas is also the day I was tossed out as a kid, forced to figure out the streets for myself. My greatest desire was food and shelter. It's why I stole. The people I robbed didn't need the extras; they had enough. But then, my sweet girl, you found me —twice. Once, you helped me. The second time, you fed me, handed me the very items I was about to steal, hid me, and then robbed from me."

"Robbed fr—"

I push a finger against her lips to stop her from talking. "You reached your little, innocent hand into my chest, twisted, and ripped my heart out, keeping it for yourself. It's been almost two months, and I've decided, between the two of us, you're the greedy one because you never gave it back. But that doesn't mean I'm not greedy for yours in return. You own me, Hayley. You have the power to send me to prison, to destroy what little happiness I want, but I'd think of no better owner."

When I finish talking, my breaths come out heavier, and Hayley looks seconds from exploding with emotion. Her hands come up to my chest before cupping my face and she inches down on the bed, wrapping herself around me.

"That was some speech, Saint."

"The fuckin' truth." Fisting her hair, I yank her head back and drag her onto my lap, right over my cock. "I'll never be the man you deserve, but I'm done running from what I want. I'm claiming it instead. Claiming *you*. I got a place, a job, now I just need the girl, and my happy-ever-after is complete."

"I haven't been the same since you walked into my life, and I don't want to start now." Her hands drop to my waist and she begins unzipping me, reaching her hand in for my cock. After a few strokes, I'm hard, and she shifts her panties to the side to open herself up for me. "You stole Christmas that night. You stole *me*. Now, you'll have to keep me."

"I can think of no better path forward. I plan on spending every holiday spoiling you. Making you as greedy as every other asshole out there because I get it now. People are spoiled when they have something to be indulgent for." I reach down for the heart-shaped pink box and rest it on the bed beside her, smiling crookedly. "Happy Valentine's Day, Hayley.

She stares at the box, emotion filling her eyes as she faces me again, holding my cheek. "I plan on giving you Christmases—*and* birthdays— worth coming home for, Saint. You'll never be walking the streets alone. We'll get a tree, and I'll teach you how to bake sugar cookies, and we'll pack our place with all the silly, bright holiday decorations. We'll have birthday cake and presents to celebrate both holidays."

Our place. She truly has no idea how much she's giving me with that promise. I'll never be stalking affluent neighbourhoods again, jealous of their holiday cheer because I have mine right here with me.

I sweep her beneath me, covering her with my body.

"Ho, Ho, Ho, and to quote my idol, the Grinch: I'm all toasty inside. I love you, Hayley."

"My thief in the night, I love you too. But it's been too long. Fuck me, Saint."

So I do, proving to her, I'm no saint.

Thank you for reading! Be sure to follow my socials or sign up for my newsletter to be notified when the next holiday novella will be dropping.

Are you a collector of all the pretty paperbacks to display as trophies on your shelves? Order your signed copy from my online store by scanning the code below:

SILENT NIGHT

ALSO BY M.L. PHILPITT

Fractured Ever Afters

A 6-book (& 2 novellas) mafia romance series of interconnected standalones based on fairytales, featuring the Montreal mafia and the New York Famiglia. Includes: enemies to lovers, bodyguard romance, slow burn, second chance, arranged marriage with mental health rep, & forced marriage.

The Bratva's Elite

A 4-book mafia series of interconnected standalones featuring the Russian Bratva. Includes: enemies to lovers, second chance, bodyguard romance, & TBD.

Captive Writings

A new adult suspenseful romance series that progressively gets darker with each book. Includes: bully, stalker, friends to lovers, & trauma rep.

ACKNOWLEDGMENTS

To all my readers! None of this is possible without you.

My betas: Megan & Colleen for our hours of back and forth hammering out the ending!

As always, a wonderful thank you to my editor, Rebecca Barney from Fairest Reviews Editing Services. Your feedback and edits are invaluable.

A big thanks to Dee Garcia from Black Widow Designs for making the cover. (She writes great books too ya'll - check her out!)

ABOUT THE AUTHOR

USA Today Bestselling author M.L. Philpitt writes both dark romance and paranormal romance. When she's not writing made-up realities, she's reading them. She lives in Canada with her four pets and survives life with coffee and an obsession with fictional characters, especially the morally grey kind. By day, she masks as a therapist, and is still waiting for her Hogwarts letter so she can be sorted into her Ravenclaw house.

Made in United States
Orlando, FL
21 November 2024

54242064R00079